The
Mixquiahuala
Letters

The
Mixquiahuala
Letters

ANA CASTILLO

ANCHOR BOOKS
A DIVISION OF RANDOM HOUSE, INC.
NEW YORK

FIRST ANCHOR BOOKS EDITION, APRIL 1992

Library of Congress Cataloging-in-Publication Data

Castillo, Ana.
    The Mixquiahuala letters / by Ana Castillo.
        p.   cm.
    Originally published: Binghamton, N.Y.; Bilingual Press/Editorial Bilingüe, 1986.
    I. Title.
    [PS3553.A8135M59   1992]
    813´.54—dc20
                                                                91-39230
                                                                CIP

ISBN 0-385-42013-7

www.anchorbooks.com

Printed in the United States of America

*In memory of
the master of the game,
Julio Cortázar*

"I stopped loving my father a long time ago. What remained was the slavery to a pattern."

—Anaïs Nin,
Under a Glass Bell

Dear Reader:

It is the author's duty to alert the reader that this is not a book to be read in the usual sequence. All letters are numbered to aid in following any one of the author's proposed options.

FOR THE CONFORMIST

Letter #	Page #
2	23
3	24
6	32
7	34
9	38
10	42
11	45
12	46
13	49
14	51
15	52
16	53
18	62
19	65
20	68
21	70
22	74
23	82
24	85
25	91
26	98
27	101
30	110
31	114
35	126
39	132
40	134
37	129
34	123

FOR THE CYNIC

3	24
4	30
6	32

Letter #	Page #
7	34
8	36
9	38
10	42
11	45
12	46
14	51
16	53
18	62
19	65
20	68
21	70
22	74
23	82
24	85
25	91
26	98
27	101
28	104
29	108
30	110
31	114
32	117
33	120
35	126
36	127
13	49
37	129
38	131

FOR THE QUIXOTIC

2	23
3	24
4	30
5	31
6	32
7	34
8	36
9	38
10	42
12	46

Letter #	Page #
13	49
14	51
15	52
16	53
17	59
18	62
19	65
20	68
21	70
22	74
23	82
24	85
25	91
26	98
27	101
28	104
29	108
30	110
31	114
32	117
33	120
35	126
37	129
1	17

For the reader committed to nothing but short fiction, all the letters read as separate entities. Good luck whichever journey you choose!

A. C.

The
Mixquiahuala
Letters

Letter One

Here's the plan:

On the 15th you arrive in L.A. i'll pick you up at the airport
and head for San Fernando, to my tíos Fermín and Filomena's
house. It will be hot, so bring plenty of baby oil (i know how easily
you burn!) and feel free to bring a bikini and shorts for tanning.
My aunt, unlike the relatives in Mexico, is cool about such things
. . . as long as my uncle isn't around.

i have to warn you about my tío Fermín. He doesn't drink too
much—he's a drunkard. He's made a point of becoming a full
fledged drunkard, so you don't have to be polite and ignore
obnoxious behavior. Like many, he will blame his weakness in
character on alcohol. If and when he gets near that point, simply
tell him, "Le voy a decir a su mujer," and you'll never see a man
get away faster in your life.

Tía Filomena has held the reins on that marriage for thirty
years. She raised her two oldest children from a previous marriage (supposedly it took place in Mexico and ended when her
husband was shot in a tavern brawl, but i have it on good authority that they were never married and he is still living in Mexico
with the wife he had when he kept tía Filo on the side) and the
two from her marriage with tío Fermín.

She took in laundry, children of working-out-of-the-home-
mothers and whipped out some mean drapes on an old pedal
Singer. At one point she did so well she had other women sewing
for her. Back in the fifties drapes must've been a big item in those
little suburban homes throughout Southern Cal.

Her children are all grown and except for my cousin Peloncito, they've been gone for a long time. Peloncito is her youngest,
and mentally challenged. He spends his days sitting in the
backyard immersed in the sweet scents of his mother's garden
and stroking a pet cat or an old dog's head. Peloncito is very

sweet, Alicia, and i don't think you should feel nervous around
him. He remembers friends and likes those who just sit with him
for a while in the afternoon sun.

Tía Filomena's oldest son stayed in Germany after his stint
in the Army. Although tía Filo won't talk about it, i happen to
know that my cousin Eddie is now Edie—if you get my drift. He
went all out, operation, the works. He was one of the best looking
men in my family too. Too bad he's not as hot as a female. (He
sent my sister a foto on the sly. My aunt would die if she knew
that we know!)

Anyway, you'll probably meet the other two cousins. Both live
in L.A.

My tía says her Chevy will make it to Mixquiahuala but i don't
know if it will be worth taking the chance. She knows something
about mechanics, but after changing a flat, checking the oil and
filling up a tank i'm lost. *You*, Nuyorquina, don't even drive,
(unfortunately there are no subways to Mexico) so i know you'll
be of little help if something goes wrong. What do you think?
Maybe we should find some other way to get back to the homeland?

There is the possibility of going with tío Chino. Tío Chino
goes home every year. He has a nice car and we won't have any
problems as far as that angle is concerned. However, tío Chino
cannot see a woman driving for anything in the world. This
means tío Chino will do all the driving, and whenever he gets
tired, we'll have to pull over or check into a motel.

Driving isn't the only thing tío Chino cannot see a woman
doing. Another is a woman gallivanting around without her
man. We don't have men anyway, you may be thinking. This is
true, and we'll get to that in a minute, but first, remember that
tía Filomena does. Despite her husband's alcoholic profession,
she has no business traveling outside a mile's radius from her
home without him—according to my uncle.

Tía Filomena's brother Chino never married. (Some say my
cousin in Germany must've inherited something from tío Chino.) The fact is, i don't believe Chino ever got it straight in his
head how to deal with women beyond the given. He was the
youngest in my ma's family and never left home, stayed living
with his mother until she died. He's very quiet. He only drinks
on weekends and holidays. Abhors cigarette smoke. (Tía Filo-

mena smokes like a fiend.) He owns his own dry cleaning business in San Diego. And he doesn't talk to women.

The trip may not be all bad, riding with lock-jawed tío Chino, but it will be a long one. Just sitting with him on the front porch last Sunday afternoon for ten minutes made me feel as if the whole summer had passed, my tío Chino and i rocking on the front porch. i said i was going in to get a beer as an excuse to get away. He said, no thanks, he already had one. i said, it wasn't for him, but for me. The look i got could've stopped a charging bull.

"Y tráeme una para mí y el niño, hija," tía Filo said, coming around the house with Peloncito by the hand. She gives Peloncito a beer now and then. She says he likes beer, but with all the faces he makes drinking it down, i think he just drinks it because it's what the others are doing and he wants to belong.

i know what you're thinking, Alicia. If Marlboros and rum and Coke weren't bad enough, now i've taken to popping Coronas and probably wiping my mouth with my sleeve after a big swallow. The truth is i just like to get into my environment. i drink pulque in the pueblitos, mescal in Oaxaca, Cuba Libres in tropical regions and beer in the Southwest—when i'm with hardy company, like my tía Filo.

Anyway, if we do take the trip with tío Chino, he'll probably ask you why you're not married. i have a sure fire answer for you, which no one in my family has dared to ask my tío Chino, so tía Filomena and i'll be hanging on the edge of our seats when you do come back with asking tío Chino why *he's* not married. And don't let him give you any bull about not finding the right one, bla-bla-bla, because we all know there have been plenty of brazen women who've gone so far as to ask him to marry—one even asked my grandmother for his hand!

Then there was the most recent case, that of the good-looking widow. Her husband left her a house in the States as well as a ranch and other property in Mexico. She was just fine for my uncle while her husband was alive, but as soon as the guy dropped dead, my uncle made himself scarce. Doña Chelito went right over to my grandmother's house, where my uncle lives, and threatened to drag his ass out in the street if he didn't come out and talk with her face to face. My tía Filomena said he slipped out the backdoor.

Doña Chelito, the grieving widow, caught up with him a week later at his favorite bar. Witnesses say she fired a gun that sounded like a canon (and about half the size!) and blew three holes in the window behind my uncle's head. She was aiming for between the eyes but, lucky for him, she'd never fired a gun before.

My tía says my uncle confided in her once that he believes aside from his saintly mother, of course, all women are possessed by the devil. "Even me?" My aunt asked, eyebrow arched, looking kind of evil-like suddenly. My uncle looked at her dead in the eye. "Especially you."

See you soon!

Teresa

P.S.

Well, going to Mexico with my tío Chino is out. He just told my tía Filomena on the phone that he is not driving to Mexico with three witches in his car.

i have another idea. My cousin Ignacio has a neat car in fairly good condition. i mentioned to my aunt that Ignacio might like to take the trip but she hasn't been talking to her son since he left his wife in Mexico last year.

My cousin's a very nice looking guy. He's been trying to get into films but i'm sure it's his dark complexion, and Huichol-like features that're standing in the way of Hollywood discovering him. Some years ago he had a small part on a TV show where he played a gang member from the barrio. He was told to speak with a heavy accent although my cousin Ignacio speaks four languages and all flawlessly.

My tía says Ignacio has become rotten like all the men in her family, picking up malas mañas from examples like his father and grandfather. My cousin claims he tried his best to put up with his wife's egocentricities, her capricious whims. He gave her all she asked for. "Including two broken teeth?" My aunt asked him sarcastically. "Especially the two broken teeth!" He answered. That's when my aunt stopped talking to him.

Ignacio hasn't been back to Mexico since the day he said the world ended for him there. His wife had looked him in the eye and said, "I don't love you. I never loved you. I only married you because you'll do whatever I say. You're a wimp. I don't even like your lovemaking. It feels like a little fish wiggling inside me! Ugh! It's repulsing!"

Bam! The two teeth went flying. He could've taken the name

calling. A man is sometimes a wimp and less when he adores the wrong woman. But never hit below the belt as this woman dared or you'll be asking for it.

Alicia, don't be shocked, but i happen to know my cousin is no pescadito. When we were children not so small but not old enough to explain our driving curiosity, we played a game called "You Show Me Yours and I'll Show You Mine." It was a simple game of discovery. What Ignacio showed me lingered in my mind's imaginings for many years after. As Ignacio grew, i tried to visualize how he must be growing all over.

Of course, it's possible that his wife knew something that i don't, which is, that maybe he didn't grow all over.

Anyway, you'll like Nacho (that's what we call him. It has nothing to do with that gringo invention of a corn chip with melted cheddar cheese on top). If i can get my tía to concede, i think he'll be willing to come along. We'll just have to keep away from the subject of marriage, which is fine with you and me, i'm sure.

At thirty, i feel like i'm beginning a new phase in life: adulthood. The twenties were a mere continuation of adolescence. But as grown-up life begins, society wants to make one believe that thirty is the beginning of the end.

i've looked for physical traces of foretold deterioration. No white hair. No varicose veins. No rheumatism or arthritis, even on the coldest of days. No shortness of breath after running up a flight of stairs. No sagging breasts or wrinkles under the buttocks. Just a few friendly crow's feet and one line where my face adjusts to a smile.

Don't be surprised at how scandalized my relatives will react to know you've never been married. (Jilted would be more understandable than never having been married.) i'll get my share too, but imagine i'll handle it as i did with my godmother, Rosaura, whom i finally went to see before leaving Chicago:

"Whatever happened to your husband, anyway? What was wrong with him? Why did you leave each other?" (She at least gives me the benefit of implying that he didn't leave me—exactly.) So many questions. Finally, i handed her a pad of paper and pen. Here, Madrina, i said. What's this for. She wondered. Write all your questions down and i'll mail them to him for you. i'm sure my husband will appreciate your interest. She sucked her tongue and pushed my extended hand with pen and paper aside.

"It is only that it was never known whether you two were divorced . . ." she said indignantly. We weren't, come to think of it, i admitted outright. "According to the Church, even if you get a divorce, you'll always be married and you'll live in sin with any other man, Teresita," Madrina told me. We didn't get married by the Church, i reminded her, who was supposedly in Mexico during the wedding but i believe had just hid out so as not to be part of my sacrilegious behavior.

We didn't even get married *in* a church, i added. We were married in the park, the one with the children's zoo, remember, Madrina? With the baby duckies, baby geese and picnickers' trash in the pond. Married by a Hare Krishna back in the days when marriages showed originality to demonstrate sincerity. It was a lovely wedding. i told my godmother. We wore flowers in our hair. "Your husband too?" She snorted. Yes, him too. We both wore long flowing white tunics . . . "How did people tell which one was the bride?" Madrina interrupted.

Back in the days when marriages were meaningful, some ten, fifteen years ago. Nothing like this new decade when young people think meaning in a marriage is a condo, or a jointly owned rehabbed building in the hip part of town, measured by how many items one owns with designers' names in bold view, a Caribbean cruise for a honeymoon and a lifetime membership in a health spa/tennis club.

Alicia, i don't know why so many of our ideals were stamped out like cigarette butts when we believed in them so furiously. Perhaps we were not furious enough.

LETTER TWO

Dear Alicia,

    Finally we end the cesspool
twirl of our 20s
that will be remembered always
untainted by today's designer jeans
camouflaged makeup, sculptured fingernails
pampered feet and glittering teeth. We
shared a jar of Noxema. In the musk halls
of a sacrificial temple at the ruins of Monte Albán
you changed your tampon
before the eyes of gods, ghosts, and scorpions
while i watched for mortals. You tolerated
cigarette smoke, tequila and brandy binges
when i was jilted on a nameless island.
    Finally men
no longer can
deposit memories of past love affairs
with their dirty underwear in our hampers. Our
art is not a hankerchief to wring out with sobs of
my man done gone and left me over and again
like a warped Billie Holiday record. (Just when
one thinks she can forget, the ass is knocking
on the door again.)
    Finally we've come to respect our privacy
slip into quiet moments with a cup of tea, a glass
of wine, reflect on the next project. Life is
balanced. Even New York makes sense.
    Was it you or me who, at 20 when we met, professed
"We're about to be sucked in by yet another decade
of unavoidable anguish and duress
the growing pains of adult adolescence

constantly afflicted with what one can expect
from a trip to Mexico: unrelieved heartburn and gas ..."
   Happy 30th birthday!

                                                Always,

                                                Teresa

LETTER THREE

My sister, companion, my friend.

   Our first letters were addressed and signed with the greatest
affirmation of allegiance in good faith
passion bound
by uterine comprehension. In sisterhood. In solidarity. A strong
embrace. Always. We were not to be separated. A fine-edged
blade couldn't have been wedged between our shared conscious-
ness, like two huge slabs of stone placed adjacent with inexplicable precision by the Incas.
   Enrolled at a North American institution in Mexico City for a
summer to study its culture and language, we were among six
young women assigned to the same boarding house clear across
the beehive metropolis from the school.
   i had worked at odd jobs for the tuition and boarding ex-
penses, only to find the school with the heavy Aztec name just a
notch above fraudulent status. My shock bored a 3 inch hole into
my native spirit, expecting to study with and under brothers and
sisters only to find California blonds and eastern wasps, instructors who didn't speak Spanish. (Is it *grazie* or *gracia*?). All this
made worse by the general attitude that no one had any objective
but to undergo an existential summer of exotic experiences.
   i'm not certain what your first thoughts were of me, studying
the dark newcomer from across the dining table, while our host-

esses giggled and fluttered attentively and with nervous apprehension about their latest American guests.

Didn't they tell anything by my Indian-marked face, fluent use of the language, undeniably Spanish name? Nothing blurred their vision of another gringa come to stay as i nodded and shook hands during introductions and took my seat.

You scrutinized me with artist's eyes: the curious manner in which i smothered avocado on the corn tortilla as if it were butter, mixed the beans with the soup of fideos, spoke only when asked a direct question, looked at no one unless it was necessary, then, it was with an air of defiance as if my presence were being challenged.

There was the mystery of the gold band on the wedding finger that struck your suspicions in a way that would show disapproval later when the fact was confirmed. i, disoriented by conceptual life, had hoped to leave it behind for the six week term. When you asked if i was married, my reply was a reluctant nod.

Among the highlights that faraway summer of our fledgling womanhood while we studied with gringo instructors who looked for meaning in life outside a commune in Idaho, and a Mexican artisan at a contemporary market geared to attract tourists with dollars—was a weekend in Mixquiahuala, a Pre-Conquest village of obscurity, neglectful of progress, electricity notwithstanding.

Its landmark and only claim to fame were the Toltec ruins of Tula, monolithic statues in tribute to warriors and a benevolent god in self-exile who reappeared later on Mayan shores, and again, on the back of a four-legged beast to display his mortal fallibilities.

We had breakfast outdoors in the brisk air, bar-b-cued tacos (the freshly slaughtered lamb steamed to perfection in a hole in the ground) thick coffee in large clay pots, and geometrically round tortillas shaped by the hands of large, squatted women with soiled aprons. Their children played nearby.

It was a visit hosted by one of the few remaining elite families in the village older than its Mexican banner. The experience, in short, took us back at least to the time of colonial repression of peons and women who hid behind shutters to catch a glimpse of the street with its brusque men.

No streetlamps, by sundown anyone with a sense of personal

safety was indoors. We spent a tense hour in the parlor until the mistress of the house (with all the gentility of one who may have come on the very ship with her forefathers four hundred years before) granted us permission to retire.

We were awakened promptly at dawn by the wretched call of a turkey propped on the wall outside our window. After a satisfying breakfast, (served by Nena, the thirtyish housekeeper indebted to the family for keeping her on after giving birth to a son out of wedlock) soured by the rude behavior of adult siblings who whined and complained throughout, a rugged hike was suggested for us along the muddy river that wound and cut through the heart of Mixquiahuala.

There, native women washed, beat clothes against polished stones; indian children with streaks of blond hair bathed and splashed carefree. At the arch of the crude bridge, a rustic cross tied with the vines of trees, marked abrupt death.

My tennis shoes were ruined and the edges of my yellow slacks were caked with mud when i lost footing and would've ended in the river had it not been for a rotted tree trunk that stopped my descent.

For years afterward you enjoyed telling people that i was from Mixquiahuala. It explained the exotic tinge of yellow and red in my complexion, the hint of an accent in my baroque speech, and most of all, the undiscernible origin of my being.

In Mexico City we discovered its ceaseless activity, the constant, congested traffic of aggressive drivers, monuments lit up brightly as if to bring in ships out of the fog, and *peñas*, student-oriented coffee houses with child-size tables and chairs, patrons with knees at their chins listened as romantic, handsome youth belted out protest songs with lungs that carried the treble of volcanoes, lyrics of lava, penetrating as obsidian daggers.

Afternoons we studied copperwork with Señor Aragón whose ten-year-old son could beat out a metal Aztec calendar in a flash before the marveling eyes of tourists; his agile hands manipulated tools that slipped clumsily through the American students' grasp.

Sr. Aragón, an adequate instructor, could be charming. He was particularly concerned with the progress of his blond students. He hardly stopped his heart's thumping over the Texan who drawled about her rich daddy and another statuesque blond with no talent but who enraptured him each time she repeated,

"No hablo espanol. I'm from New Jersey," repeated New Jersey as if he were deaf rather than not comprehending where New Jersey was. He didn't like you. And he didn't like me.

You had your ever firm ideas about design and had already taken sculpture classes in New York.

i, with dark hair and Asian eyes, must've appeared like the daughter of a migrant worker or a laborer in the North (which of course, i was). i was nothing so close to godliness as fair-skinned or wealthy or even a simple gringa with a birthright ticket to upward mobility in the land paved with gold, but the daughter of someone like him, except that he'd made the wade to the other side.

His oldest son, Gilberto or Roberto or something, tried to court you on a bench in the plaza. His inexpert kisses tasted of Marlboros. He whispered he'd marry you if you'd go off with him to a friend's room.

In the evenings in our room at the boarding house, we laughed. This, above all, i've treasured in having known you. How you made me laugh behind the closed door, away from critical strangers. You mimicked Gilberto or Roberto and his proposition. It was the slobbering kisses that had refrained you from going off with him some afternoon. We made light of his pompous father who charged us for each piece of copper we used while believing he'd been sly enough to give the blonds all but his eyeteeth without our noticing; and how he'd grown indignant the day a tourist asked to buy your work!

You told me of your lover, Rodney, back home, with the yellow eyes, how you once contemplated having a baby, just like that, knowing your future with him had been predetermined by societal mores. You astounded me with your casual references to a slew of nameless lovers who'd served your sexual whims.

i learned of your mystical dreams with the one you had when we first met. You were the ocean, immense and horizontal, your hair the tide that came in to meet the shore. You watched as i walked alongside you, head erect, dressed in torn muslin, a small bundle tightly pressed against my bosom, unaware of the trail of faceless male figures in slow pursuit.

Now i think i know how you saw me that first summer, although at times i was ethereal to you. i was part of the culture that wouldn't allow me to separate. You, on the other hand, saw yourself isolated, even unwanted by men and their world, observed me from that reality.

Your cries, like the roaring tide, didn't reach me. You wanted to warn me against my predators, but i couldn't understand the abstract warning of nature.

Perhaps you recognized my strength, an element in my character that would readily stand defiant, but was also coarse like the muslin. Sometimes i was vulgar and my courage misguided.

You were speechless when i was escorted out of a nightclub in Chicago after having swung at the rude barmaid, and interceded diplomatically on another occasion when i shoved a large brute who obnoxiously laid a hand on my rear.

If that strength could be nurtured so that the emotions i wore on my sleeve were tapered, you sensed i might become a dynamic rallier of womanhood. Instead i lashed out at inappropriate times and cowered when it would've been best to respond with dignity.

We were filled with vivacity for scooping up life, enjoying it to its fullest. Why was peace of mind so intangible?

The other women who stayed at the hostel—the sixteen-year-old blond from California whose parents were to meet her on their yacht in Mazatlán at summer's end, the one with the face of an Ivory soap commercial, who was to marry her childhood sweetheart after college—were they *happy* because they had no need to question irregularities in the way they were treated? Had they survived the summer in Mexico by not becoming part of its heart-wrenching/spirit-drenching madness?

At the end of the school term, we made loose plans to return to the United States, hoping to venture a weekend in Acapulco beforehand.

My husband came for his selfish wife, embittered by shame or embarrassment for her not returning dutifully after the privilege of running off on her own for two months.

i was the flicker, flame, butterfly ablaze, my husband's bride who wanted to fly in search of mythical rainbows beyond the rain. i was marked by something good or evil, but that would never leave me.

It was apparent i was no longer prepared to face a mundane life of need and resentment, accept monogamous commitments and honor patriarchal traditions, and wanted to be rid of the

husband's guiding hand, holidays with family and in-laws, led by
a contradicting God, society, road and street signs, and, most of
all, my poverty. Its drabness.

i had so much more to fight against than you, who ran desperately to find love in strangers' arms, secretly sought approval
of your bigoted father, knew undoubtedly that one day your
work would be accepted by the status quo because you were its
new generation deliberately shaping its forthcoming tenets.

You fell in love with an Indian caretaker. My husband and i
fought like vicious enemies. We left each other, flew back on our
own. You stayed to pursue an idyllic affair. Summer came down,
clashed hard against us who had ended in resenting each other
because of our desperate acts.

Each time we've parted it has been abruptly. We picked,
picked, picked at each other's cerebrum and when we didn't
elicit the desired behavior, the confirmation of allegiance, we
reproached the other with threatening vengeance.

Each time, a few days passed, a week, and i'd receive a copy of
Neruda's poetry, you, a ten-page letter of self-recrimination,
you, a long distance call in the dead of night, i, a hand-painted
postcard, you, a copy of the *Diary of Anaïs Nin*, i, a pair of copper
earrings from your recent collection, you, seven poems fresh out
of the typewriter, i, a ceramic brooch.

We begged for the other's visit and again the battle resumed.
We needled, stabbed, manipulated, cut, and through it all we
loved, driven to see the other improved in her own reflection.

Letter Four

Alicia,

Do you know the *smell* of a church? Not a storefront, praise the Lord, hallelujah church, or a modest frame building with a simple steeple projecting to the all heavens, but a CATHEDRAL, with doors the height of two very tall men and so heavy that when you pull one open to enter you feel as small as you are destined.

You were never led by the hand as a little girl by a godmother, or tugged by the ear by a nun whose dogmatic instruction initiated you into humility which is quite different from baptism when you were annointed with water as a squirming baby in the event that you should die and never see God face-to-face because you had not been cleansed of the sin of your parents' copulation.

It smells of incense, hot oils, the wax of constant burning candles, melting at a vigilant pace, the plaster of an army of saints watching with fixed glass eyes, revered in exchange for being mediators and delivering your feeble prayers. It smells of flowers and palms that precede Easter. It smells of death.

The last time i went to CHURCH, genuflecting my way to the confessional, i was eighteen years old.

i was a virgin, technically speaking, a decent girl, having been conditioned to put my self-respect before curiosity. This did not satisfy the priest, or should i say, stimulate his stagnant duty in that dark closet of anonymity and appointed judgment.

He began to probe. When that got him no titilating results, he suggested, or more precisely, led an interrogation founded on gestapo technique. When i didn't waver under that torment, although feeling my knees raw, air spare, he accused outright: *Are you going to tell me you haven't wanted to be with a man? You must have let one do more than . . . than what?*

i ran out of the booth in tears and in a rage, left the CHURCH without waiting to hear my penance for absolution of my unforgivable sins.

Always,

T.

LETTER FIVE

Alicia,

You told me once, we were on a palm strewn beach in Puerto Rico, i believe, (i recall the gold-tooth peddlers and the old men weaving *pajas*) that you were taken to Spain when you were a small girl.

Your grandmother, on your father's side, was from Andalucía and part gypsy. She sang, with a spine-tingling gutteral voice, lyrics you never understood but felt just the same. There was one melody, a lullaby, that your mother learned and sang to you on nights when the demons that search for children hid under your bed. "*Este niño no tiene cuna. Su papá es carpintero. El le hará una.*" This child has no cradle. His father is a carpenter. He will make him one.

You told me that gypsies are an oppressed dark people who nevertheless live celebrating death through life. That was all you knew about gypsies.

The beach became empty of sound, though children kept bobbing playful heads above the waves ignoring mothers' reprimands. The sun was white and transparent against its blinding glare. We said nothing more. You went on to sketch something. i lit another cigarette.

Your parents had never wanted anything to do with that mongrel race, the lost tribe, and fought in America for American ideals and the American way of life.

We flipped the sand that rippled between our toes and looked around at the mimosa of Puerto Rican faces, making a mental note to ask your parents what those ideals had been.

Teresa

Letter Six

Remembrances on a January day when a constant shiver has taken hold of my weary bones:

You fell in love in Acapulco. Adán was the Indian caretaker of an unoccupied hotel newly purchased by the ambitious Tabascan whom we'd befriended at a Dairy Queen. That was where, within a few days, we parted ways.

From the dusty bridal suite of the linenless bed, uninspiring cobwebs and roving tarantulas, one had a breathtaking view of the bluest sea for an immeasurable expanse, an orange sun that dove slowly into the horizon at dusk.

Our host bar-b-cued steaks by the barren pool, glad to have our company, i suppose, engaging us in singalongs and behaving like a kid at camp. There was no electricity or running water. We were glad to sleep there rather than the alternative of a rogue-possessed beach. By candlelight we each found our way to a room for the night, like phantoms, called to each other out of the blackness to give a point of destination.

After three nights, we thanked our host and went on our way. You opted to remain, enchanted by the haunting beauty of the deserted hacienda, the virile lover of skin like polished wood, and the hypnotic sea, just as the summer ended and the season when sharks come in with the tide began.

One cool afternoon in September back in Chicago, when my husband and i had settled into our banal routine, you called from the airport.

Your utopic affair had ended, smashed to death like a scorpion against an adobe wall. Adán's wife had arrived from the village with their children. The wife you didn't know existed. You kicked him hard in the groin, attempted a crude karate chop across the neck in a rage, threw his love songs composed on balmy nights into the aquamarine ocean for the sharks to bleed, pulled off the strings to his guitar and tied them around the straw mat on which he had first taken you.

Tourists know of a different Acapulco, one of skydiving, gliding through the air, water skiing, dancing to rhumba music on marble terraces, English-speaking guides and colorful, bargain-filled markets.

Our Acapulco was of Mexicans who were black and kinky-haired with shackled history, grease-covered mechanics, people who watched us slyly with unsympathetic notions of our vaga-bonding, and Adáns who wondered what it would be like to make love to the infamous North American white woman so transcendental that a wife from the village should've been inconsequential.

In my apartment, with its second-hand furniture, the black cat called Salomé, books and onyx chess set, faraway from the ocean, scorpions' stings, and lying lovers, you drank a special tea to induce your menstrual flow. Your feet were cut and calloused. You painted watercolors while i was at school, ate in silence. Then you went home. Our first summer's odyssey had ended.

It was possible that we might have never seen each other again. So much was possible then.

Tere

Letter Seven

Poor Alicia,

A high school diploma in art, no marketable skills and such depth of loneliness that you spent the winter refuged in your bedroom in that wonderful home of your childhood. If you didn't look out at the greyness of the suburban street and only painted, you wouldn't have to face the disoriented future you'd begun to create.

You wouldn't have to think of Rodney, your boyfriend from Harlem. Rodney, always down or high on something, who never kept an appointment on time, remembered to call, or told the truth unless it was to his advantage.

So your passion poured itself into watercolors, pale and removed, like the memories of a few luscious weeks in Acapulco, a brown-skinned man who'd sung lullabys in a native dialect and told folktales of his righteous ancestors. It would've all been relegated to your powerful dreamworld had it not been for one letter.

He probably wondered for a long time afterward, since of course there had been no return address, where that scribbled envelope he had mailed so far away would finally rest.

He might've imagined a woman, as pale as you, but older, with hair the color of straw in the sun (not black like yours since you inherited your coloring from your Andalucian grandmother) and her eyes would be the color of the sky on a troubled day. She would climb the stairs (like the ones he saw in a Pedro Infante film when he first moved to Acapulco) to your room where you'd be at the window, sobbing now and then into a perfumed hanky, nursing a broken heart.

His fantasy wouldn't have been all that absurd or out of bounds with reality because, in fact, it had been your mother who'd brought up the letter; her eyes are the color of the sky when it's about to storm, and you had sobbed with a broken heart, onto your sketch pad if not into a hanky.

The Indian who had played lovers' games with a complacent wife and a hot, young gringa would've found it all as glamorous as the film he'd seen long ago because this scene would include him as the star.

Did you keep the letter after reading it twice, under your pillow, or in the bureau drawer with the mementos of your adolescence? Did you take it out nights when you couldn't sleep or paint, or when Rodney had stood you up in the subway, and wistfully hope for the Indian wife's death so that you might return to your paradise niche overlooking the sea and embraced by the sky?

At the start of the new summer you picked up and took the bus to Chicago, pallid and all tied up in a knot like a pretzel from Central Park.

It was not destined to be a particularly good summer for either of us.

i took my final exams and finished at the university. You stayed with me in my mother's flat, sleeping on the floor of my room. She wasn't pleased a second daughter had split with her husband and we tried to keep out of each other's way. Stones of silent condemnation were thrown from every direction, relatives and friends who believed "bad wives" were bad people.

My husband had moved to California, a move that held more promise than being unemployed without a goal or aim in Chicago. One would've thought i'd sentenced him to hard labor in Siberia.

For all our summer had not been, we managed to have our special days because we were bound in that yet undefined course known as The New Woman's Emergence.

At a pier, i read poems and passages out of books aloud while you painted and commented that the lake seemed immense enough to take us as far as China.

My mother had only been close to female companions during her adolescence. My older sisters never maintained close relationships with women after marriage. When a woman entered the threshold of intimacy with a man, she left the companions of her sex without looking back. Her needs had to be sustained by him. If not, she was to keep her emptiness to herself.

We included in our clandestine chats and activities the sister who'd dared to declare a separation from her husband of a decade. We invited her dancing with us, to view avant-garde films, picket supermarkets, and she went eagerly.

She was enthusiastic about all our suggestions because for the first time in her life she had a choice, expressed an opinion and was able to decide what she wanted to do on a Saturday night.

What we could not offer my sister was acceptance into society, her raison d'être. At the end of the summer, she went back to her husband. i packed a duffel bag with jeans, poems, and a few books, and went to follow mine too.

Always,

T.

Letter Eight

Alicia,

Do you remember that tepid afternoon in Washington Square? What was that pimp's name? As if the name mattered as the essence of the conversation, or rather, his eloquent monologue.

There were in fact a few pimps who approached us on that occasion, curious about the two subdued women who soaked in the last of the summer sun, jeans rolled up to our knees, shoes kicked off.

You were undoubtedly sketching something, and i no doubt smoked a cigarette. We wrapped up all our thoughts we had ground over the summer like Colombian coffee beans, hoping to come up with a resolution that would make the future tolerable. On the bureau in the guest room of your parents' home lay a plane ticket to California.

Again, i was the deserter, giving up Woman's Quest for Freedom and Self Determination. i was on my way to my husband, stopping off in New York to spend just a few days with you—as if postponing a sentence to Siberia.

i must've been saying something about this, you pretended to listen, although you'd heard it all before and kept on grinding that old number two into the pad. Maybe i said something like: "This time everything is gonna work out between my old man and me. All i'd needed was a little time to 'grow up,' finish school, get some curious energy out of my system." California was a place to start over, grow together. No, i didn't want any children. i was still a child myself. i probably laughed at this remark, as if it were meant to be a joke.

Right about then this fool pimp, kind of decrepit like, came over flashing some cheap piece of jewelry, talking about it being something genuine from Mexico. We said nothing in response, did not even smile or frown at his ridiculousness. When he failed to get us to bite the bait, he went on his way.

It was the young pimp with the charismatic smile, cruising on a European ten speed, the kind that were hot and trendy, that i recall. He was smooth, wasn't he? His rap was like smoked glass, hand-painted by Chinese artisans in a sweatshop. Slick but repulsive for its exploitation.

He never once said i had pretty eyes or a sweet figure. Instead he suggested my potential from a business angle. "See that woman over there?" He pointed to a working girl with a flashy style. She wasn't going to get anywhere. Never once did he suggest that the type of business was fatal. It was all in the approach.

You listened, the way you do, glancing up now and then from the sketchbook. "How old are you?" he inquired. "21." "What do you do with yourself?" He asked next.

"Not much."

"Not much, huh?" He reiterated for emphasis. i nodded, not much. Do you work or go to school? He wanted to know, probing deeper. i shook my head. What inspired me to encourage him was perhaps something like boredom. Perhaps i was amused. No, i didn't go to school. i lowered my head for effect and added, dropped out in the seventh grade. *Seventh grade?*

i looked up. The sun behind his head was a halo, a big grin all over his face. He took a seat next to me.

He began to explain his business strategy: in a year i could save one thousand dollars. i could then open a business of my own, a beauty parlor if i liked. One had to work with an objective he advised knowledgeably.

He himself was getting ready to do the same, having been able to save a substantial sum. He went on like this, occasionally shaking his head at the prostitutes going by, commenting that they'd never get anywhere because they didn't have the know how or someone to guide them. He asked if i would have dinner with him.

i declined politely.

i was on my way to San Francisco to join the last of the flower children, but thanked him just the same. He smiled and got on his bike. As he sped away he called over his shoulder, "In case you don't make it to California and I see you here again—we'll get together!"

i made sure i didn't go back to Washington Square.

Always,

Teresa

LETTER NINE

Alicia,

Since we met that summer in Mexico you believed i'd no business being married, eyed my wedding band as if it were a shackle, found it incomprehensible that any woman of your generation could willingly commit herself to slavery. i don't think i ever told you the story of when i reached the crux of my dilemma and finally made a break for it:

We were living in California. As anyone with eyes and a nose could tell it was a haven for all those who dared to dream.

Libra, as he was known popularly, had wandered for the six

months he'd been there on his own until he found a quaint town where he thought we could settle down and as the proverbial idea goes, live happily ever after.

He had never finished high school, but what he lacked in formal education he made up for in street smarts. Or so he liked to believe. The huge ratio of people to any one job brought Libra to conclude the only job he would ever have was the one he made for himself. We decided to go into business

or rather, we agreed Libra should go into business and along with Edwin and Jr., two Latin types from the East Coast, our pennies were invested in a body shop.

While Edwin and Jr. claimed to have established the base from which all their dreams could manifest, they had only one aspiration all along: Jr. wanted to win the Golden Gloves Championship and Edwin, as his manager, would get him there.

Libra, caring about his business partners as he did, being a man and therefore understanding the importance of such an aspiration didn't complain when he turned out to be the only one of the three working in the shop.

He didn't complain when Edwin and Jr. made sure he gave them their two-thirds profit at the end of the month.

He didn't complain when his entire shop was vandalized and his associates looked at him as if to say, "Well, we all know *you* were the only one working. It must've been *your* fault someone was able to break in and take *our* stuff!" He replaced it and kept on maintaining the shop with little more than a helping hand and an occasional visit from Edwin and Jr. who were busy training for the next fight.

He didn't complain when the entire shop was vandalized a second time. His associates looked at him as if to say, "Well, dumb fool, whatchu gonna do now?"

So i complained.

i complained day and night, week in and week out. i kept the books and scowled at Edwin and Jr. each time they showed up with their hands out for their share. Libra kept right on working until one day he uped and quit, said i had nagged him enough. Edwin and Jr. agreed. The three went off to the gym to train Jr. for the next fight.

The little money that came to us after the equipment had been sold bought us an old MG. Libra loved to cruise down a mountain road, blue ocean below, wind blowing through his

curly hair that came to his shoulders . . . Sometimes he gave me
driving lessons and for a while we lived off my modest income.

Jr. didn't win the championship and with Edwin returned to
Philadelphia. Can't say i missed them, but they did leave a trail of
broken-hearted divorcees and married ladies.

One of them, who had taken Edwin in and put up with most
anything from him was particularly scornful and came by to see
me one day after he'd gone without so much as a good-bye.

She'd been drinking and brought along a half empty gallon
of cheap wine. We sat on the front porch, drinking out of plastic
cups, watching her kids dig up bugs beneath a walnut tree.

"How come Libra let those two bums get away with what they
did?" she asked, letting out a loud belch. "Oh, you know how
men are," i said, having wondered the same thing. "They were
his friends."

"Friends don't rip each other off," she spat and eyed me with
the look of a hardened woman who was out for blood. i stared
blankly at her. She went on. "Who do you think broke into that
shop anyway—crooks, gangsters?"

She took a swig from her cup and finished. "We ain't got no
crooks or gangsters in this town . . . no more that is!"

Some time passed, maybe months or only weeks. Libra made
a new friend and associate, Melvin Oates. Melvin was tall and
solid as a brick wall, black from California sun and with exqui-
sitely carved features. He was a man's man, or at least, Libra's
idea of a man, an expert in martial arts, well read on all the latest
cults, a self-proclaimed philosopher with a strong yen to draw
timid souls to bend to his liking.

Melvin convinced Libra that a surefire business that wouldn't
infringe on others' rights to breathe fresh air and live wholesome
lives was to become street vendors. They could purchase a horse
and wagon and sell fruits and vegetables as was done years ago
and still in some places in the South.

Libra and i drove way out to the country to a farm where a
man was selling his old work horse that had been retired years
before. Melvin and his main lady, a tiny Laotian woman named
Cristina, hitchhiked out there to meet us.

"Yes, this old horse has still got some good miles in 'im. This is
the one for us, Libra," Melvin declared, stroking the decrepit
animal on its last leg as if it were Secretariat. "Pay the man,
Libra," Melvin ordered. i took one look at Libra, bit my tongue

and walked back to the MG. After his experiences with Edwin and Jr. i was certain Libra wasn't about to embark on a similar joint effort.

Cristina came over and stood by me while the two men talked business with the farmer. Shortly, the farmer walked away. Libra and Melvin came with the news. "We're picking it up tomorrow," Melvin beamed, and gave me a look of defiance. i may have been Libra's wife with considerable influence but Melvin was a man and a man's woman could not compete with that.

"We'll meet you all back home," Melvin said to Cristina and me. The three of us stared at him. "Libra and me are riding back together. We're partners now and we got business to discuss."

"What're you talking about?" i asked Melvin, my blood seething. "Aww, c'mon, woman. Don't give Libra a hard time now. You always talkin' 'bout being equal to men, being able to do anything a man can do, don't tell us you afraid of hitching home!"

Libra studied his sneakers, shuffling them into the dirt. It was my fight. i walked away, aware of Cristina's soft steps following behind. A good ways down the road after the MG had sped past, i stuck out my thumb.

Monday, while Melvin and Libra were getting that old horse, i packed my duffel bag with jeans, books, and poems and moved out on my own.

Always,

Teresa

LETTER TEN

Alicia!

In mid-January the sea is a perfect green
folks buzz 'round doin' their individualized and collective
thing pass out leaflets on 24th & Mission churn out dough for
meaty tortillas fry sweet bananas get their steps together
for the dance Saturday night & the salsa band
from NY
silk screen posters in every shop window:
                    Palmieri
                        Barretto's
                    comin' to
San Francisco, man!
photographers and poets record the beat of low riders women
paint walls with their own history. Hills and trollies right out
of Riceland Rice commercials and my God, so many Chinese
all knowing the secret of immortality (which is in their greens
or tai chi)! Fields of vines forever—bittersweet grapes pulsate
with the very heart of the industry count each one and it's not
worth a dime but a day's labor will feed a family of ten one
more day.   Lethargic afternoons analyzing Viet Nam shell-
shocked vets putting together vacant ends sharing
rice and beans babies and information tapes for public radio
alerting workers of the world to unite:
Buenas noches y welcome to "Somos Chicanas," a program about Chi-
cana women by Chicana women, for Chicana women. This evening we
are very fortunate to have in our studio a poet from Chicago, a Chi-
cana who has come to share some of her work with us . . .
        (An epidemic of nervous giggling takes over the
sound room, the engineer switches off to a Joan Baez tune,
snarls at the twelve women crowded around three mikes.
When they are composed he cuts the music and turns us back

on. We break up all over again—back to Joan Baez.)
   Motorcycle rides
along jagged mountain sides delivering contacts for jobs
government forms and spiritual massages
                        in the back
holding on for dear life to a mexicano brother with a red
bandana tied 'round his brow and two quarts of beer in his
gut
   lots of names
Alicia, do you remember?
Not just names, but names of long, lost kin
husbands lost to immigration officials taken on a bus
and never heard from again
they were cousins
The eloquent scholars with their Berkeley Stanford
seals of approval
all prepped to change society articulate the
social deprivation of the barrio
                      starting with an
Anglo wife, handsome house, and a Datsun 280Z in the drive-
way
       they were our new brothers
Remember the clannish Samoans and Pilipinos of the Spanish
surnames mysterious smiles and strange clothes?
They were baptized by the same godfather i pierced
the left side of my nose just above the nostril wore a black
pearl perpetually
donned dungarees, bandana to keep my head from toasting
but gave such a genuine farmworker Pomo look Anglos
kept waiting for my bowed head to know my place on
public streets
but i didn't of course being from
                    Chicago the hawk
the windy city that gave Dr. King the lowliest reception outside
Memphis
        Ignorance
didn't scare me in 1976
      Year of the Bicentennial
we were in Dolores Park
among the radicals of the day gays feminists painted red

circles 'round bare nipples watched it all like
a documentary in progress
                              a parade goin' by
Observers,
            never invited to participate sensing ours
was to record not immerse in time
TIME IS FLUID
                  We call it by name: ... 1974, '76, a moment
of Southwestern influence, our Aztlán period

                                          TIME IS FLUID
The days are eternal dry hot a drought began water
measured precious oil   We call it January, June
autumn leaves constant green
                        Wonderland
lay back trip out on street mime clowns jugglers peddlers
of invisible magic dust sometimes in a barren apartment
we roll back the rug and dance
                        made up our own steps before the
eviction when we pack books typewriter pots in crates that
served as tables mix a paste of flour and water stick a giant
poster of Geronimo on the wall reads: LANDLORD but before
then we made tortillas in the sun-spilled kitchen one mixed in-
gredients another rolled out geometric round with the instinct
of hundreds of years practice a third turned them on the
comal . . .
                              There were three of us then,
remember? You me the childhood friend from back home
whose husband called every morning at 7 a.m.
hating that she left
"to find herself" as was the order of the day
We were obsessed
with visions of snakes that threatened
to wind themselves around our yearning hearts . . .
      and we formed a society of women a sacred triangle
an unbreakable guard from a world of treason deceit and
                                          weakness.

                        Teresa

LETTER ELEVEN

Dearest Alicia,

When i say ours was a love affair, it is an expression of nostalgia and melancholy for the depth of our empathy.

We weren't free of society's tenets to be convinced we could exist indefinitely without the demands and complications one aggregated with the supreme commitment to a man.

Even greater than these factors was that of an ever present need, emotional, psychological, physical . . . it provoked us nonetheless to seek approval from man through sexual meetings . . .

You lay flat on your belly
a coarse rug painted red irritation but you would
not complain
closed your eyes and waited
                    for the circling patterns of
his expert fingers
first against the temples to erase fear
instill trust
you relaxed
then the shoulders a few turns of the joints and
with an acrobat's leap to the back
down the delicate spine for a long time along the back
oil burning into your melted flesh electrified
                    fingers undid the bra
for a moment you were aware of yourself
lay very still alert and awaiting
                    kept the pose
all barriers had been cast away
                    he kneaded
the small hollow of your lower back
you let out
            an almost inaudible moan

the elastic waistband of your panties
pushed down over the swollen profusion
                                        of your buttocks
with the help of his confident hands
worked past thighs horizontally
                                        clumsily
over calves and each naked foot
on the sofa
                        across the room
i closed my eyes
                        went on
                        with my nap

                                                        T.

LETTER TWELVE

Alicia,

of prophetic dreams, not a Pisces, sign of mysticism and premonitions, not one to assume power except that acquired by your curiosity of the laws that guide men.

Yet there was the recurring dream throughout that Californian summer, of Rodney, whom you'd left to apartment sit in New York:

You returned from your trip and found another woman staying with him in *your* place. Putting aside or having chosen to ignore the drafting table with its color pencil box and pastels, half-finished watercolors tacked sporadically and without rhythm save your own, Moroccan wallhanging a relative had sent on a birthday long ago, high school yearbooks, your mother's porcelain soapdish, given up only after a great deal of nagging on your part—and had made it *their* place.

Both sat at the small table by the window, high above the

traffic and booming population, sad about a secret shared and held close to their navels, each one.

Her hair was braided tightly about her head and it was her Afrikan blood that haunted you most. She was not his deceased mother, you were sure of that, far too young, and an ambience of sensuality flowed between them.

The sight stunned you into immobility. They didn't look at you, even long after the first seconds since you entered the room. It was as though they were in mourning. The air smelled of gardenias that made your stomach rumble like a stirring volcano and you ran to the bathroom to rid yourself of the eruption.

One stifling night, when the vines rustled melodically and crickets sang in monotonous harmony, you awoke in a sweat from the dream and on impulse called him. You knew he was not alone, in your room, on your bed (carried into the city by your father). The patched quilt your Spanish grandmother had brought on the ship tossed carelessly on the floor. It was the same foto of Rodney on the nightstand inscribed, "To Alicia, Forever Yours, Rodney," but it lay face down.

Somehow you saw it all through the window of dreams' enigma.

He was groggy, aroused from a deep sleep and at first despondent to your long distance call. All you wanted to know was, was he alone? Answer me, Rodney. Is anyone there with you? The fragment of silence that preceded his negative reply told you. The firm no meant nothing.

We talked in the morning, over camomile tea and succulent oranges. You looked for wisdom from an old sage and i feigned confidence about the endless possibilities regarding that telltale pause.

Still, the warning of the dream did not lure you back
to Rodney
your lover since the age of sixteen.
While his father got wasted at a bar
the tiny red stain on a grey sheet
made you his.
If he stood you up for a party on Friday night
left you waiting in the subway station
forgot your birthday and Christmas
year after year
you forgave him.

He was a poor, misdirected, deprived black man from
the ghetto
and you, the privileged white girl of the suburbs.
Laid so much guilt your limbs lifted themselves
with lead weights around his back and tears came
when he went away that he would never
see never
never see.

(There are a dozen proverbs we could interject here. Your
mother shook her head, arms folded over her chest like an
impenetrable fortress. Your father pretended that you didn't
associate that closely with any black man . . .)

It was cold in Manhattan when you arrived with souvenirs
and sketches to piece together the months of vagabonding
throughout the Southwest and Mexico revisited. It probably
hadn't snowed. The streets, dun colored, the way they are in New
York in November and in cities infamous for alienation of the
human heart.

No one had come to meet you at the bus depot. You did the
rare thing of catching a cab to the tenement, out of fear of
getting mugged with such tempting cargo, odd objects wrapped
in newsprint that protruded from brightly colored straw bags.

There were five flights of stairs up to the door with the three
bolted locks and peephole.

It had been a long journey home, so long that you were in no
rush to get inside, more so because you knew you were about to
enter not your apartment but transcend from one reality into
the other.

For a split second you thought to run, give *her* a chance to
collect herself, whatever she had brought with her, leave your
home, change the dream before it became an actual nightmare.

Each lock turned slowly announcing your return. You
thought you heard something stir inside, but you hadn't. Time
had stopped.

You remembered later, much later, noticing first how thin
Rodney had become, long and lanky, legs stretched out under
the table by the window, appeared like an obscene giant insect.

You never saw her face, just as in the dream, turned away and
lowered so that you involved yourself with the intricacies of those
fascinating braids, so much more fascinating than in the dream.

You swallowed hard and thought it sounded like a plugged

drainpipe in the somber soundlessness. Your stomach was empty. There was no perfume of gardenias. You didn't feel the urge to run to the bathroom.

Your legs and arms were useless and the bags dropped like anchors on the unwashed linoleum, the pattern of which had faded a generation before.

Forcing yourself toward the bedroom, like an astronaut on the moon, slowly lifted one foot, then the next. The bed hadn't been made and the sheets were musk odored, but you lay down anyway, and closed your eyes.

Remembering,

T.

LETTER THIRTEEN

Alicia, why i hated white women and sometimes didn't like you:
    Society had made them above all possessions
the most desired. And they believed it.
My husband admitted feeling inferior to them. The conquest
would break matters even
permit him with his head up
                                arm in arm with his dough colored
i hated
white women who took black pimps
everyone knows savages have bestial members
i hated
white women who preferred Latins and Mediterraneans because of the fusion of hot and cold blood running through the very core of their erections and nineteenth-century romanticism that makes going to bed with them much more challenging than with WASP men who are only good for
                                making money and marrying.

And i hated white
men even more. It is probable and i admit that somewhere in
my genes runs European ancestry (although no one in my
family has bothered to trace further back than the Mexican
civil war when my grandmother chased behind Pancho Villa's
troops to swoop up her son in Torreón and ended up in a
bleak place called Chicago).
                                        Since it isn't obvious without family trees
or in the narrow slits of Mongolian eyes, i've never said it. i ate
meals with tortillas and fingers, a peona by birthright comfortable without chair or table but squatted.
Mexican peasants can no longer afford cornmeal but
i'm getting off the subject which is why
i hated white women.   You knew when we first met
sensed it all over my Antarctic pose: i didn't want to be
your friend—you, some WASP chick or JAP from Manhattan's
west side and we could not possibly
relate.
But i was only half right. You were partially white
raised moderately comfortable
spoiled by mommy and grandma if not by daddy
half as egocentric as i suspected.
that's not to say that *not* being comfortable, white or an
only child made me less concerned with myself. i found
sources to direct my anger
pointed at them
called them white
privileged
and unjust.
Meanwhile, you were flat-chested, not especially pretty and
bore no resemblance to the ideal of any man
you encountered   anywhere.

Letter Fourteen

Hermana,

i wish i could have convinced you how beautiful you are, then perhaps you might not've gone through so much personal agony during that second journey to Mexico, or at other romantic times.

i'm not referring to that inner beauty one goes on about with diplomacy and discretion as consolation for the absence of external attributes, ever critical to women beings.

i am in fact speaking of that which to no credit to ourselves we have inherited by genetic combination from the precise moment when our fathers' and mothers' seeds meet.

Let us take inventory.

You keep your virgin hair long, long, a snake hung by its tail down the narrow ripples of your vertebrae. Putting antiquated values regarding feminine beauty aside, it *is* lovely. You know that. That's why you keep it, brushing fastidiously nightly like a weaver of precious silk.

But that isn't your most admirable asset, while you've confided in me that you don't believe it so, your legs, the angular lines of your body at once reminiscent of a child transforming into a woman, in this day and age society bestows an approving eye.

Why don't you see that?

Why do you shun the plum breasts, the raisin nipples that stand perpendicular to your torso—as if nature deprived you of a harvest?

You, the artist, must've observed in the mirror, the graceful curve of the slender neck, as you tilted your head just so when embarking on a new sketch.

The pianist's elegant fingers with the simple silver band of abalone on the middle finger of which hand i forget.

That's the secret of your beauty, subliminal, momentary, a

sunrise, a sunset, a cyclic experience for the one who bothers
with infinite details, awaits suspended at the onset of the sym-
phony for the first moments when all the musicians tuck violins
under chins with stirring patience watch for the conductor's
baton to begin.

i, the poet, never praised you lyrically, instead scolded to put
an end to your timid inhibitions; i've imagined it's done no good.
They were only the words of another woman.

LETTER FIFTEEN

So Alicia, as you may reluctantly recall:

California ended one summer day. The separation from my
husband, the meager salary from a part-time job, the eviction
out of the apartment, all pointed to an unavoidable exile.

There was a definite call to find a place to satisfy my yearning
spirit, the Indian in me that had begun to cure the ails of humble
folk distrustful of modern medicine; a need for the sapling
woman for the fertile earth that nurtured her growth.

Ever the butterfly, not spared of mortality, and California
could offer no more than an end if i stayed.

No aimless rambler, or total free spirit that could be blown in
the wind's preferred direction, i searched for my home, be it a
cave alongside a barren cliff, a ranch of chickens and pigs, a city,
with a multitude of familiar faces confused as hungry as me. i
chose Mexico.

Books and curiosity gave me substantial reason to seek the
past by visiting the wealth of ancient ruins that recorded awesome, yet baffling civilization. i planned out a route: afterward, i
would settle in Mexico City.

Our "love affair" was at its height and the idea of the journey
that would lead from ruin to ruin offered your creativity new

dimensions, so before returning to New York—of course, you joined me in the new adventure.

Not so long ago, as we rinsed out late night tea cups, yawned and scratched, prepared for bed, when i stopped to see you for a few days on my way from one place to another, you mentioned *Mexico Revisited*. Wearily, you muttered, never having been able to pull apart its entanglement in your memory. You sensed, in the end, it all had to have meant something, that, if we were able to analyze, it would be pertinent, not just to benefit our lives, but womanhood.

i nodded, alert, having already begun to open the sealed passages to those months. "i'm writing about it," i confessed. You shuddered, went to bed.

LETTER SIXTEEN

Alicia,

Ours was a relationship akin to that of an old wedded couple. While we might agree on a basic plan or idea, all else had to be bickered out. i doubt if what i'm going to recall for both our sakes in the following pages will coincide one hundred per cent with your recollections, but as you make use of my determination to attempt a record of some sort, to stir your memory, try not to look for flaws or inaccuracies.

Rather, keep the detachment you've strived for since knowing, if you kept it close, it would go on hurting. This isn't a tale of our experiences, but of two women who

had a rendezvous one Sunday at precisely three o'clock, in the square of the quaint Mexican town neither had ever been to before. Knowing the colonial design of Spanish architecture, we knew there would be a square.

i arrived the day before. As the second class bus turned the last mountain curve to reveal the picturesque town drawing gringo artists and hippy types during that era, i felt at once transposed back in time.

The cobblestones, the women washing clothes in public basins (a kind of laundromat without machines), the white, wrought iron benches skirting the plaza. At its center, the proverbial kiosk where musicians hit their cymbals and blew trumpets in worn uniforms every Sunday afternoon, and, of course, the imposing cathedral erected centuries before when the world was destroyed and a new one begun.

Vehicles weren't allowed through the streets of town so i took my bag and walked the two or three blocks from the bus depot to the square where i took a seat and waited.

Alvaro Pérez Pérez was a colleague from the school i'd been teaching at that summer in California. Mexican, he was short, and built like a compact bull. He worked as a substitute teacher at the school, his diverse background ran from home economics to the martial arts. In a pinch, he conducted English classes although he spoke with an outrageous accent splattered with Chicanismos, one could only assume was not done with some intention.

Alvaro Pérez Pérez was a self-proclaimed healer, an alcoholic, and in love. i wasn't fully conscious of the latter that afternoon while i waited for him or had chosen not to think of it. Instead, i remembered riding with him via motorcycle throughout the vine country of Northern California, seeing to the needs of undocumented workers, the ill and the destitute who had crossed the border in search of a better life.

We were drawn to each other by the Indian spirit of mutual ancestors. It hadn't been an immediate alliance to be sure; his drunken scenes at faculty meetings, his eccentricities, and demonstrations of a violent tendency were all but encouraging for a woman who took her politics seriously.

He sought me out, in the grand stubborn fashion of the Mexican man, and finally i believed that beneath his rebellion was a sensitive human being with an insight that was unique and profound. (This is a woman conditioned to accept a man about whom she has serious doubts concerning his legitimate status with the human race.)

There were long talks that wound themselves into insomniac nights. Alvaro Pérez Pérez was a volume of many tales that one could listen to and find some truth in to take into another day.

Above all else, there was our intense devotion to the culture that had preceded European influence.

He invited a few of us to spend some days on his father's ranch outside of that dream inspired town, and as we had already decided to make our way to that country, we accepted the invitation.

i sat on the bench for perhaps a quarter of an hour, my eyes darted apprehensively to the huge clock on the steeple, wondering if he would appear or if he had gotten himself involved in another incredible adventure. At last, walking ever so leisurely, wearing a pair of dark glasses and the same pair of dungarees as when i last saw him, he approached the square. As if Alvaro was doing nothing more than taking a stroll, with complete nonchalance, he sat next to me without a word.

We said nothing for several minutes. Our minds weighed like ripened fruit on the branch. When one is confronted by the mirror, the spirit trembles.

In due time he began a monologue of his latest escapade, which dealt with the roundabout way he returned home. (He'd been in the U.S. without papers.) He'd hitched all the way to Acapulco. It even included a free ride on a charter plane. Acapulco was out of his way and as he attempted haphazardly to reach a closer proximity to his destination, he ended up back at the border, where he was apprehended by the authorities for not having proper documents. (His faculty I.D. obviously wasn't considered a proper document.) A two week stint in prison was utilized to unite his fellow inmates to make specific demands regarding the deplorable conditions.

He led me on a tour of his hometown, which also served as an account of his biography, the colonial house with the boarded, louver windows, where he was born, the tiny cemetery with cobwebbed plots where he and his cronies had played hide and seek, the primary school where he was taught his alphabet.

i was fatigued and lugged my bag that held all i'd deemed necessary when leaving my life in the U.S. He was aware that i was tired and the bag heavy but continued the game of tour guide maintaining a peculiar, almost antagonistic distance but i tolerated the inexplicable obstinancy.

It was dusk. We went to the house just across the square. Upon entering a long courtyard, beyond a wooden gate, there were doorless rooms along each side and at the far end, a dark, claustrophobic kitchen.

In one room, his older brother prepared *hongos de maíz* (your favorite Mexican food and a weakness you couldn't resist despite the diarrhea suffered for days after), dogs nipped at my heels and hens scattered feathers as we passed.

His sister-in-law, a light-skinned, boisterous woman sat in one of the bedrooms with a small child on her lap. He left me with her and went off. i didn't ask to where. She read one of those romance magazines laid out comic book style with the exception of using real photographs.

"Does he beat you?" she whispered. In her mind, being left in her care, we were immediately in league. i blinked. She assumed i was Alvaro's new woman and looked at me with admiration. She explained:

Alvaro was the youngest of his father's sons, but because Luis Felipe, her husband, had defied his father by marrying a woman of "ill repute," Alvaro stood the only chance of inheriting his father's property.

Understandably, she assumed we were lovers but conformed to formalities by inviting me to spend the night in the guest room, informing me that Alvaro took the small room just above the kitchen.

She told me in the morning i would have the pleasure of meeting Alvaro's parents who came to town for Sunday mass. She always sent her children with Luis Felipe, but she never attended.

Night had come quickly and i prepared for bed in the stark room. Within a short time, Alvaro appeared. He didn't knock. In fact he came through the window off the balcony. From behind his back he produced a mango the size of which i hadn't seen before. Isn't this what you said you craved for back in Califas? i smiled. As he peeled back the skin, releasing the exotic juice, he entertained me with another of his fantastic stories. Then he left me to sleep in peace, unlike the blood thirsty mosquitos that stayed.

In the morning, i indeed had the opportunity to meet Alvaro's parents in the square after mass. (Neither Alvaro or i had the inclination to attend the services so we had waited outside.) His father chose to ignore my presence altogether which was more kind than his mother's treatment.

She decided i must be a tramp, like the one married to her older son, that i was out to get my greedy hands on her husband's wealth. When i rebutted, informing her that i was but a colleague of her son's and was in the country for other reasons, having only come to that town, like other friends we expected, upon an invitation, she grunted.

Waiting in the square that day, i was anxious for your arrival. But you didn't show up at three o'clock.

Two other friends, a pair of lovers, came and the four of us decided to wait (actually, *i* was the only one who waited) in the small cafe across the square, opposite the brother's house. Periodically, i went out to scout for you. Meanwhile, Alvaro guzzled beer after beer with his friends.

As dusk fell, the ritual that echoed and haunted young romances for centuries began. The male, usually accompanied by friends, went around the square in one direction, the female, usually accompanied by chaperones, walked in the opposite. A strange mating dance of the higher species. A band of aging musicians serenaded the promenade from the kiosk.

Alvaro and the lovers drank heartily in a festive mood of reunion. i, too, had my glass or two of brandy but never lost sight of the planned meeting.

i'll never forget the laugh i had when finally i spotted you, going 'round and 'round and no less in the same direction as the men, towing your knapsack over your shoulders. But we were joyous to see each other, weren't we? Then and there in the face of prim pretense we hugged and jumped about in each other's embrace.

It was when we returned to the cafe and i saw an odd expression on Alvaro's drunken face that i sensed trouble. It was all there, knotted in the twine of his brows. He'd hoped you wouldn't show, but you had, and for a few minutes, he pretended to be glad.

He took us to his brother's house. i started in the direction of the room i was inhabiting but he tugged to lead you to the other room, the one above the kitchen. We began to argue and he pulled me aside, leaving you and the other two awkwardly standing among nipping dogs and chickens in the dark courtyard.

He wanted to spend the night with me. It was that plain. To a drunkard, it was plain. To me, it was ridiculous and i said so. That's when he declared himself in that honorable fashion of men of my culture. He wanted me to stay so that we could be together always. His father would find employment for me, if that was what i wanted. He loved me. He had a right to spend one night with me.

i told him to forget it.

He left then with the two friends, angry, cynical, and laughing loudly through the unlit streets like a spoiled adolescent.

We knew Alvaro Pérez Pérez well enough to anticipate we hadn't heard the last of him that night. Part madman, part fool. We pushed the small writing table with the chair on top to block the door. Then we undressed and went to sleep.

It was some time later, or so it seemed, when the loud screech of the table being pushed away by the opening door awoke us. What is this? He taunted, knowing the precise reason for our barricade. It had been to keep the mosquitos out, we both replied ludicrously, pretending to be casual about his intrusion.

In the shadows, we saw him throw off his jeans and shirt, and climb into the bed, with me sandwiched in the middle. Within seconds, we were bombarded by his exaggerated snoring interspersed with farting.

Alicia? i whispered, holding my breath. *Can you sleep?* Instantly, his snores stopped. He listened. *No,* you answered. We got up and attempted to pull the cover off but he clung on, his snores grew louder, animal-like, vindictive.

We crept downstairs. The sounds of creatures moving about and restless in the dark shadows of the courtyard were frightening so that we hurried back up to the room and spent the night lying on the cement floor, close to each other to keep warm.

In the morning, Alvaro Pérez Pérez arose, seemingly refreshed, although i suspect he had a hangover. We, like a pair of dogs, huddled at the foot of the bed.

Downstairs in the kitchen, while we had café con leche to get our blood flowing again, we announced we were leaving. He said nothing but disappeared.

As the bus we boarded pulled out of the depot, we scooted down, out of the window's view, in case a sniper took aim to embed a bullet in the head of the woman who had no interest in the Pérez estate—or its heir.

Love ya,

Tere

Letter Seventeen

Moving right along . . .

The Story:
The medical student i'd met the summer we studied in Mexico City was still living with his family when we found ourselves needing a place to stay a year later.

Ask me why he dramatized hurt and offense over my not returning immediately after i finished at the university. He'd declared his love that summer.

No need to get worked up. i had returned.

His mother, who had always displayed a polite affection for the North American friend of her ambitious first-born, welcomed her—and her traveling companion, initially. She chose to believe i was a kind of exchange student/pen pal of her son and he encouraged the misconception.

Like any good son, he was devoted to pleasing his mother. He was the ideal son. His parents had bought him a car and gave him free room and board believing, in a short time, he would become a doctor, the first professional in the family.

On the first night of our reunion, parked on the corner of the apartment building where they lived, he cried in my arms. No, he practically wailed, a raveled ball of self-pity soaked my bosom. He confessed he hadn't completed his studies and indeed wasn't doing his internship as his parents believed. He had neglected his studies and failed exams.

He cried because he feared the inevitable when his parents would find out. i had no advice for him, apathy kept me from interceding.

Sooner came the time when his mother gave us strong indications that we had overstayed our visit, being that, in her eyes, he and i were at best only long distance friends, and as it was clearer by the day that he didn't take too well to you, she saw no reason for our staying.

One occasion when we were blatantly snubbed by the mistress of the house was the night the entire family went to a fiesta and she made it clear it was for relatives only. Thus, we were left behind in the apartment to plan our strategy once leaving the present accommodations.

You sketched. i smoked. We spent some time trying to count up your lovers, but kept losing count until we got sleepy and went to bed. Should i say, to floor—since that is where we were allowed to sleep. We threw our trusty sleeping bags down on the floor of the daughter's bedroom.

We had long gone to sleep when the thud-like clumsy sounds of the family returning from the party stirred me awake. A few minutes later, i heard his voice, just outside the room. He seemed to be talking on the telephone, using an abrasive tone he never practiced at home. He made demands, accusations of noncaring, unfaithfulness.

"This jerk's talking to a woman," i said to myself and put on a bathrobe. Tiptoeing to where he stood wavering in his drunken state, holding the telephone receiver to his ear with one hand and the drink he'd carried from the party in a styrofoam cup in the other.

Why was she reproaching him? He demanded to know just as he caught sight of me, arms folded, a sentinel before him.

Who are you talking with? My voice was not particularly low. It didn't matter if the whole household got up. i'd had enough of the country where relationships were never clear and straight-forward but a tangle of contradictions and hypocrisies. Let the mother be the first to hear . . . !

"A fellow intern . . ." he stammered, an obvious lie. Grabbing the telephone from his hand, i put it to my ear in time to hear a woman's voice. i hung it up, and went to bed.

The Verse:

Past the wrought iron gates
swallowed by 16th century
deteriorated sanctum
the keeper, half asleep
or drunk,
took the pesos and tip
the key out of the wooden box
and led the way

She smelled mold and age
in the courtyard
behind the series of locked doors
the muffled silence of 2 a.m.

The near finished bottle of tequila
the wilted rose, crumpled pack
of cigarettes left on the bureau
His keys and wallet he tucked
well inside a pocket

In the bathroom
a face cloth and a sliver of soap
The bare bulb on the ceiling
hurt her eyes

They made love
fast
imitating tradition
He would not allow himself
to dream but turned
a freckled back to her presence

This was her last night
in the homeland
of spiritual devastation

In an hour they would tiptoe
past the plants, reupholstered
furniture aware that beneath
the crucifix, on a flat pillow
his mother sighed:

Her son would not leave her

Letter Eighteen

In Mexico

you said i'd acquired the body most desirable to men of the
region. i scoffed at your remarks, enjoyed tacos in hot sauce,
generous portions of rice and beans, brandy and Cokes, and
didn't want to consider how they affected my physical appearance.

You ate with a greater appetite, and found it difficult to keep
up your weight. That was just the way it was, i simplified, ex-
plaining individual metabolism. Having the choice, i'd prefer
yours, i added.

Men's glances on the street, their apparent pleasure when
eyeing me told you that skinny was fine for high fashion but did
no good when what you wanted was to appeal to men's passions.

This obsession climaxed during our days in Oaxaca, where
we passed to see the ruins of Monte Albán. We took a bus to the
Zapotec ruins of crumbling glory, but refused to be led by a
guide and set out on our own. After a bit of exploring and
pyramid climbing, we found a cozy spot out of the penetrating
sun and rested on the smooth stone.

As always, you pulled out the sketch pad and watercolor
pencils. The inspiration was awesome but i couldn't respond as
immediately with a poem and satisfied myself with the snapping
of pictures.

A young man, a local, also with a sketch pad, introduced
himself. He was drawn to your work, the skillful reproduction of
hues and angles, the capture of the dream-like quality of the
surroundings.

We talked casually about the Pre-Conquest culture of warriors and their militaristic sense of architecture, all the while you
never ceased drawing. Impressed with your talent, he was anxious to make friends. He couldn't praise you enough. Gracias,

you said modestly, scarcely raising your eyes from your work.

He pointed to a beaten VW parked on the side of the road and offered a ride back to the city.

You took the front seat.

At the marketplace, we ate tacos while he continued to lavish attention on you, asking questions about New York, and your artistic goals. Uncharacteristically, you began to relax. You told yourself that he was interested in you, the woman, Alicia, the person.

His hair was wild and he was dressed shabbily. He managed to charm you since he appeared at the ruins.

i contented myself independently, delighted with the montage of the marketplace, the doves and parrots in wooden cages, handmade wares, Zapotec women in bright, shiny skirts, hair bound and hidden beneath grey rebozos.

The new friend said only one thing to me. It was about the time i finished a series of tacos. *Gordita.* Undaunted by his remark, i ordered another.

You were curious about his work and we went to his studio a stone's throw from the market. His paintings were amateurish and unexciting. You hoped for something from his amiable personality and your expectations built.

When night came, we sat on a wrought iron bench in the main plaza, like lost waifs, with nowhere to go and not much to say to each other. We observed the couples out for a stroll and those playing courting games as they passed each other circling the kiosk.

You anticipated his move.

Instead, without warning, he turned his attention to me. Unlike his manner earlier, which had been informal and easy, it was tense and somber.

He spoke rapidly in whispers, his back almost directly to you. i didn't even listen, agonized by your sense of rejection.

Finally, you spoke up. You wanted to go back to the hotel. He escorted us without protest and offered a ride to the bus depot in the morning.

In our room you were sullen and despondent. i took out a photograph of my husband and me on our honeymoon and reminisced aloud about expectations, evident by the grins, arm-in-arm by a motel swimming pool. i said that men were tiring me, although my fatigue had come from interactions with one in particular.

You refused to have your shield penetrated. You steamed your face over the bathroom basin (a practice we began while traveling to maintain a healthy complexion).

i confronted it. What is it? Did you actually care about that guy? You didn't even know him! He's just some poor jerk with not much to offer! He can't even paint!

i bit my tongue. You gave him that fine watercolor of the ruins in exchange for a work that never materialized that day. (After seeing his work, i didn't suppose you minded.)

You couldn't bring yourself to look at me, who stood defiantly. Then, lifting your face up to the dull mirror, "You . . . just . . . don't . . . understand . . . Do . . . you?"

No! i lied.

The next morning he came by promptly, with his mother, an old Zapotec woman who only spoke the native dialect and donned traditional costume. (This impressed the hell out of you, so fascinated by the unrelenting customs of the fierce people who never gave in.)

At the depot, he asked me for a lock of hair. You gave me a suspicious look when i allowed him to cut it. Wasn't i the superstitious one who warned against leaving hair, clipped fingernails, photographs and personal items where they might be used to do one harm?

He put the hair inside his billfold and his mother said something which of course, we didn't understand. We asked. He almost smiled. "Just good luck . . . and have a nice journey!"

We boarded the bus and rode off without looking back.

i'm sorry, Alicia,

T.

LETTER NINETEEN

You wanted to decipher one day,
you said,
as we stirred our stoneware cups with star of anis and earl grey,
what it could've meant. There was distance in your voice and you
were pale in the amber glow of the nightlight (kept on in the
kitchen for those trips to the communal bathroom out in the
hall in one's half sleep) or because it was winter. You're always
pale in winter.

Five years had passed since our return.

The days are long and angular, Alicia. When the suffocating
heat is broken by a welcomed thunderstorm, i can't help reach
out, fingers grope in the summer thick air. Something in the
food odors collected in hallways, the waddle of the pregnant
woman who passes below my window, the smell of dead fish and
chemicals that rises from the lake and is wind blown toward the
houses on my street make me nostalgic for that place.

Mexico. Melancholy, profoundly right and wrong, it embraces as it strangulates.

Destiny is not a metaphysical confrontation with one's self,
rather, society has knit its pattern so tight that a confrontation
with it is inevitable.

When we returned to Mexico together we met our destiny at
every stopover, pueblo, city, cafe, on any bus, street, at the coast,
peninsula, and central plateau.

The reason it was so blatantly painful, to the point that it
made you cringe at the sound of the male voice, was that we had
abruptly appeared in Mexico as two snags in its pattern. Society
could do no more than snip us out.

How revolting we were, susceptible to ridicule, abuse, disre-
spect. We would have hoped for respect as human beings, but
the only respect granted a woman is that which a gentleman
bestows upon the lady. Clearly, we were no ladies.

What was our greatest transgression? We traveled alone.

(The assumption here is that neither served as a legitimate companion for the other.)

And travel we did, down, down, for days and nights, among the chickens, rancid food, odors of unwashed bodies, bus after bus until at last, we arrived at the Yucatán Peninsula. *Pedazo de América*, as the Mayan poet we encountered there described it.

The weeks we spent living in semiluxurious self-indulgence at the hacienda of the entrepreneur.

Mornings, when the sun was at its high point, we sunbathed by the pool, sipped on guayaba drinks, made small talk with his eminent friends. My presence and sudden interception in his life never interrupted the rhythm of his daily affairs.

Most of the day he was gone, returning in the heat of the afternoon to eat and take a siesta as was the custom. i wouldn't see him then, or rather, wasn't allowed to see him. Instead, it was in the evening, when we dined, met with friends on the patio by the pool, or when he came directly to my room.

He had invited us to make his home ours. His staff was at our disposal, no one ever questioned a request but considered it an order.

At night, there was spontaneous festivity. His friends returned, refreshed and smelling of enticing aftershave. There were libations and lighthearted conversation. Sometimes, we danced to the music of the trio he had hired for our exclusive pleasure.

There were other women, whose presence he casually explained as business associates. They sought consultation regarding investments, and so on. They were lovely, wore strapless dresses and hair cut in the ultimate French coiffure. None was a local woman, but from Belgium, Switzerland, or some other exotic place.

But Sergio Samora, grand man about town, the sole person in charge of his family's wealth was not interested in such women, only in their investments. Hadn't he toasted to the incomparable bronze skin of the tropical woman? All his friends reached high up with filled glasses and smiled with open admiration at my indigenous heritage.

Of course, i know now what a mockery that was.

You were enraptured by our seductive surroundings, the

aromatic guayaba trees growing in abundance in the garden, the nimble-legged flamingos dipping beaks in the pool, the slew of handsome lovers . . .

Among them, an owner of a factory in Veracruz, who was hardly a day older than us, but having inherited his father's business, pretended to be the mature sophisticate.

Ahmad, of black, lustrous hair and eyes more somber than a child's promise, dressed in Italian shoes and tailor-made shirts, never a hair out of place or a crinkle in his slacks.

He invited us to his home in Veracruz. When we declined, he persisted. Sergio, my entrepreneur-suitor, thought it wasn't a bad idea, and coaxed us to accept. It would allow us the opportunity to see the first city founded by the Spaniards.

Sergio was charming and forever attentive, showering me with attention. Within no time at all, he proposed marriage and went on to elaborate in detail our entire future. i had landed on a strange planet where cares and worries did not exist.

He would buy una casita, a little house; we wouldn't live in that huge hacienda with so much traffic and goings on. On our honeymoon we would tour Europe and visit Japan where he had business. In two years, precisely, we would begin our family.

i'd always be at his side, his assistant, his interpreter. (i would be sent to study other languages.) i would oversee the administration of one of his businesses, (pick one).

Sometimes, when the guests had left and i went to my room, i paced the floor with its rose-colored tiles that kept the room cool during the humid night heat. The fan twirled with a melodic hum from the ceiling.

At last, i revealed to him that i was married, but that my leaving the United States was an act staged to determine its end. He wasn't pleased about this news, nor that i wasn't a virgin. He professed sincere love, however, and he would see to it that i got a divorce.

It would be quick and quiet, none of his relatives were to know. We would be married immediately afterward. i asked if i might be allowed to send for my family. He insisted on it. i sent a letter to my mother and her reply (which came with unusual rapidity) told me she was ecstatic. Finally, i was redeemed. She, too, would take precautions to make my present marriage seem as if it never happened.

i thought of the city i'd been brought up in, where dark skin and a humble background had subjected me to atrocities. The children that i'd have wouldn't know that persecution. They wouldn't suffer at the hands of the ignorant, but would be raised in a land where copper-colored flesh was the norm. They would never know a day of need. Above all, they would have a sense of belonging.

i was never in love with Sergio Samora, although he was attractive and likable. What did love have to do with the order of things? A woman didn't marry for love in that part of the world. She married out of necessity.

In the modern U.S., i married a poor man out of love. Poverty had won out and separated us. i was of the multitude and survival and its perversions were ingrained. i had been instilled with cynicism and, very soon, the only door opened to me to escape the banal destiny planned from birth
exploded
into a billion splinters of sheer farce, without a sound.

LETTER TWENTY

My protégé,

Let us now speculate on the everpresent existence of an underground network of ongoing activities that the public is never quite aware of, busy boarding buses, running shops, manning machines. An eyebrow raises at the dinner table, the head cocks at the broadcaster's announcement on the car radio. A country's government has been overthrown at dawn by its military; a major strike of miners, truck drivers, telephone operators has metropolitan areas at a standstill; protestors have burned down the flag of an embassy, then become human swiss cheese to the entire police force or army. We go on eating rice and beans, driving along to an inconsequential appointment. It has nothing to do with us.

Occasionally, we hear a commentary. How little human life is worth. Yes. The sum of years of accumulated memory ended with the meeting of a bullet and grey matter.

It was hurricane season. The summer months had passed and September was halfway gone when we arrived in a particular city by the coast. Leaving our hotel and going to catch a bus to the main square, a white compact car with three men passed. They whistled and called, but we refused to acknowledge them.

'Round and round they came, relentless. When we reached the bus stop, it had begun to rain, a relief from the torrid heat at first, but then it poured mercilessly. There was no place to go for shelter and we stood like wet ducks firmly grounded on the corner. When the men in the white car pulled up to the curb and inquired where we were headed, reluctantly we told them but refused the lift. They sped off.

Two brutes sensed our vulnerable dilemma, we were drenched in green rain, and began to harass us. We were frightened. The white car came around once more. One of its passengers called out, "Sister, get in!" Without a second thought, we jumped in, ironically, gratefully.

i sat up front with the driver and two were in the back with you. They seemed friendly enough and asked our names. i recall when i turned around to reply and saw the heavy armaments that could be used for nothing but warfare, i let out a gasp. You were pale.

Having a better command of the language, i responded to their questions, but they detected an unfamiliar accent. "Are you North American?" They wanted to know. i tried to laugh, as if the suggestion was ludicrous. How could they possibly think that? Couldn't they see by our color that we weren't gringas?

It's the blue jeans, one said, as if stating a statistical fact.

For some reason—instinct, perhaps—caused me to deny that we were, but thought it best to admit we were foreigners. They then named a South American country as a possibility of our origin. Yes! That was where the accent was from no doubt! How were matters down there—since the military takeover? They asked eagerly. i muttered an ambiguous reply.

The roads leading out of the city were all blocked, they told us. The authorities were looking for two individuals who had made an attempt on the upcoming president's life the previous day. Two women and a man. The man had been killed trying to escape. The women disappeared.

As we listened we felt their scrutiny. Our minds raced with collages of blood-ridden thoughts, newspaper articles, pictures of dead guerillas, decapitated villagers, North Americans taken hostage, shot with machine guns against church walls.

We were expected downtown, i said. My mind spinned with ghastly images. We were only passing through the city on important business.

Two blocks later, we were dropped off. The white car sped away. Until we were back at our hotel, we hardly uttered a word.

Just another pretty face

LETTER TWENTY-ONE

¿Sabes?

Nearly a month has gone by since i began to remember the Yucatán saga. The conclusion must be the cause of this heartburn and not the chicharrón in hot sauce i had three weeks ago. To be rid of it, i must create distance:

Un cuento sin ritmo/Time is Fluid

The two women arrived on the first ferry that morning. They were bombarded by a dozen urchins wanting to carry their bags, direct them to the best place to stay, eat, swim. None got the chance, nor so much as a smile.

The sea was sapphire, a fluid orchid. Sea birds swooped and skimmed along its surface. Men, whose gold-capped teeth caught glimmers of sun as they gave pitches for a great day at the Garrafón, swallowed the women with their black unfriendly eyes. No one heard the women speak. They didn't smile. Behind

a wall of opaque glass, they were left alone
          but were watched from a distance, followed. Boys called
to them. "Hey, gringas! ¡Oye, chula!" The men who leaned
against entrances to the souvenir shops snickered, elbowed each
other and whispered, threw obscene kisses in the air.

The women didn't see this. They didn't hear. They were
protected by an invisible amulet, a spiritual guardian whose
great wings enfolded them as they trudged over the hot sands.

One wears faded blue jeans rolled over the ankles, the other,
army fatigues; both have bandanas to hide their hair. Their bags
are unstylish and show wear. A woman pulls her small child back
into the cafe where she cooks, casts a cynical look their way. She is
glad she's not them. Still she wonders, her eagle squint says.

The days were long. There are three, not evident by a calendar or newspaper but by the three identical suns the women
witness rise each day before they take the ferry away from the
island.

There are voices everywhere, but they are unintelligible
sounds, not syllables that form words, messages, but sounds just
the same, a grating sound that blends with other sounds blended
with that of the sea that eventually becomes a single drone.

It isn't obvious that the women have little money. It is obvious
that they're foreigners and typical of the youth of the day, travel-
lers rather than tourists. It isn't surprising that they stop at the
first shabby motel they pass.

A young man, perhaps only seventeen, shows them to a
room. A girl, with a watermelon belly and an infant perfectly
formed but tinier than an elf who clings to her skirt, hides
behind a door and watches her husband take the womens' bags
to the first of many empty rooms along the stretch of sand.

Once the curtains are drawn and the women are left alone,
they undress and rinse off in the shower that has only cold water.
They put on swimsuits and carefully hide passports and travelers' checks under a loose tile on the floor. They have done this
without saying a word. They do not even smile when they're
alone.

Out in the blaring sun they choose a road, any will lead to the
sea. The one with the legs of a male adolescent, ahead. She
jumps rocks, occasionally stops to examine something that has
crashed with the waves against the jutting rocks of the sea. The
other goes steadily. She's not agile, but robust, full.

There are words between them, not many, but one will speak
and the other nods her head seriously. What do they say to each
other? How intimate they are! What language do they speak?

One picked up a dead branch and lingeringly drew something in the sand. She drew a snake. S. She draws another snake.
S. Two snakes. S.S. She was obsessed with snakes. The snake
woman, Coatlicue.

Her companion formed a visor with her long-fingered hands
over her eyes and examined the construction site of a new hotel.
She frowned, or her eyes were sensitive to the sun. She watched
for a long time.

For hours no one has seen them. Did they dine at your place?
Did they turn up at the disco? Do you suppose they returned
from wherever they came? A waif claims he saw them. They wore
dresses and their hair, like silk, hung long like mermaids' hair,
blew ghostly in the salt wind. They were at the dock, sitting,
perhaps waiting, but met no one on the last ferry.

The following morning they were the first at the bank. The
management apologized but it could not exchange their travelers' checks. Hadn't they heard on the radio? The peso depreciat-
ed overnight. No one had arrived at its current rate of exchange
and the bank couldn't make the transaction until then. Don't
worry, the stout manager with the Pedro Infante moustache
assures them. You'll just have to wait. Enjoy yourselves until
then.

They return to the dock, eyes focused on the incoming ferry.
After it has docked and all its passengers spilled out, they turn
away. Caught in the crowd of newcomers they are approached
again by the men who own motor boats and take parties out to
the Garrafón.

The excursion includes lunch of fresh redsnapper and ceviche from conches just picked from the sea. There's a swim
among the colored fish, and snorkling. The redsnapper one
guide will catch is promised to be twice the size the next will
catch. The women shake their heads.

One of the men runs to catch up with them. Your credit is
good with me, he tells them. Each woman turns to face the man
almost nondescript. He was nondescript because at once each
woman knew he was detestable. His meaning was apparent. He
may have had the worth of a slug at best.

Your credit is good with me, he repeated.

Why, one of the women uttered.

Why, the second one uttered. Sí, ¿por qué?

You can't go anywhere until you cash your checks, he answered confidently. The women followed him to his boat.

He'd caught two customers but he needed at least six to make the tour worthwhile. Leaving the women, like conches he dived for to prepare ceviche, he went off to round up the rest.

The sun was pungent. The women reclined on the boards used for seats in the small boat, an arm over the face to protect the eyes. The drone began. It drove into the ears like a screw until their heads throbbed.

Ah ha! So he's going to take you out today? It is the voice of the waif separating itself from the drone. Each woman uncovers her eyes to lift her head. The waif is a silhouette against the sun. He laughs.

What's wrong with you? One woman utters.

Why are you grinning? The other woman utters.

Their voices are monotone but the waif knows they were irritated. He continues to grin and jumped off the boat laughing like an imp. *He says you're not paying with money!*

That evening, along the horizon as the sun exploded, one saw two motor bikes carrying passengers, circling the island, along sand hills, past the Garrafón, the ruins, sixteenth century dungeons sealed off by iron grates, beaches where men waited for turtles to come in with the tide when they bludgeoned them to death.

The men brought the women back to the hotel. The women thanked them and motioned to go their own way. Won't you have a drink? One man's invitation was heard over the sea's warnings. The women declined and went in the direction of the beach, lit now by the moon and the amber lights of the nearby hotel.

They found a smooth stone where the sea foam rose and fell, and sat together. One played with miniature crabs that slipped between her fingers and toes. They were like the ones she'd known in the Atlantic as a child. The familiarity made her smile. The other smoked a cigarette.

There is laughter somewhere in the shadows. The laughter of the waif, hiding, watching. Come here, one woman demands. Now what? The other woman shouts toward the shadow. The waif comes forth.

Those men, the urchin giggles.

Which?

Those from the docks, the ones you were with today . . . the boat men. They're getting drunk at the dock now. They're saying they had you both.

Get away! Go! The women demanded angrily, impatiently.

Back in their room, they feel the night has eyes, a voyeur, behind drawn curtains, cracks in the salt-eaten door.

It went on like this, Alicia, you know, another day, another night. The drunken men on the beach, whose voices were heard gaining on us. Still unable to cash our checks without money, we slept on hammocks in a hut where land crabs, blood-sucking mosquitos and any natural or unnatural creature of the earth may have come to strangle our silly necks.

¡O juventud! ¡Divino tesoro! My mother quotes from a favorite poem. Oh, youth! Divine treasure!

i don't want to go on with this story. You know the rest.

LETTER TWENTY-TWO

One early evening as we strolled through the square of the whitest and oldest Spanish city we had yet visited, we were drawn to an outdoor cafe by the lively sounds of marimbas and guitars.

We took a table to have a cool drink and write postcards. "i love you, i love you, i love you, i lo . . .," i scribbled on the back of one for Sergio, not meaning it but wanting to affirm that i would return to the Yucatán; while we continued to traverse unfamiliar terrain, there was an immediate place to call home.

The air smothered even as dusk settled and the lights along the plaza came on. Men of sun crisp skin and white shoes drank brandy and talked gregariously; assorted trios of musicians with pasted smiles serenaded from table to table, a song for a price; women posed in chic, revealing dresses and nonchalant gazes. We had arrived at what seemed to be in comparison to the other towns of our journey an extroverted and ultramodern metropolis.

We were timid because of our foreignness and tried our best to remain as inconspicuous as possible, as if our presence suddenly discovered might cause our new surroundings to vanish. There was hardly a word exchanged between us. Months of miles of moving continuously away from the familiar had worked their evil on our minds and emotions.

Each day you withdrew deeper into yourself. You suspected that the invitation from Ahmad hadn't been sincere and again, we had been duped. Leaving the Yucatán and detouring to Veracruz instead of returning to Mexico City as originally planned, because of a supposed opportunity that was doubtful, had made you incensed and bitter. There was little to say to each other.

We were so engrossed with our detached observations that we didn't realize we were also being watched and had become the topic of conversation for the two men at the next table.

One, who seemed the younger of the two, came over. "My friend and I have a wager," he said cheerfully, as if he had known us for years. "He says that you girls are South American. I say you are gringas."

I cleared my throat, examining the tall, amiable character as coolly as possible. You didn't so much as glance up. "What makes you think we're gringas?" i asked, trying not to give away defensiveness. "Easy. Your blue jeans," he replied smiling.

My eyebrow shot up for dramatic effect, running my eyes over him he became conscious that he too wore blue jeans and was presumably no gringo. "I just came back from a business trip to the United States," he said by way of explanation. He had a boyish charm that disarmed my guard. "Anyway, which is it? The loser pays for all four."

i felt the stirrings of a new mood. There was the opportunity to have an easygoing conversation and i said, "It seems we win either way, so we've no reason to tell you."

i got up to join them and you followed without altering expression, robbed of interest in the present, you were absorbed with one thought. You would find Ahmad in Veracruz. You were a zombie and in no state to befriend anyone, particularly men. We ordered a couple of sodas and sipped from paper straws.

If one could rely on instinct at all, although it is a primary resource for survival, i sensed the two men were somewhat dif-

ferent from the ones we had recently encountered. They didn't
ask the usual superficial questions or lavish us with pretentious
flattery. Instead, they told of their work for the state as engineers
with engaging enthusiasm.

A large house had been provided for their living and working quarters. The house was relatively new, not more than five or
ten years old. They hadn't known who had owned the house
previous to the government. In the months they'd resided there
some peculiar occurrences had been taking place leaving them to
conclude quite frankly that it was haunted.

A chill ran down my superstitious spine.

You didn't wince. Your mother had spared you a religious
upbringing. Your father was a dogmatic atheist. Nothing you
couldn't see and touch existed.

i, on the other hand, having been raised by a spiritual healer
grandmother who'd believed in the metaphysical way of the uni-
verse, couldn't shake off the idea that ghosts existed among us.

i admired your apparent annoyance with their talk, not susceptible to fear by accounts of shaking beds, bodiless shadows,
hollow footsteps in the dead of night. Two foreign women who
had come to do some work for the government had taken one of
the bedrooms over the summer. Their bed had trembled at night
and once had actually risen from the floor.

A sense that these accounts were genuine made me uneasy,
while you remained indifferent externally, staring past us, waiting, always waiting for one moment to transcend to the next,
bringing you closer to your objective . . .

Shortly, a third companion joined us and immediately fell
into the discussion of the unusual occupant who could not be
seen but certainly heard and felt. He attempted to validate their
stories with one of his own:

I fell asleep one night on the couch downstairs . . . I was very tired
from working all day, you see. Suddenly I was awakened by a loud
thumping coming from one of the bedrooms upstairs. I ran up to see what
it was; I thought someone was having a fight or maybe it was a burglar.
The only other person in the house was Luis (the guy who'd invited us
to their table), *and the noise was coming from his room. I tell you, my*
hair stood on end like this when I saw what I saw! He was sound asleep,
but his body was elevated in the air about a meter from the bed! The bed
was shaking up and down . . . then, before my eyes, it stopped, and Luis'
body came down slowly back on the bed. He never awoke during the whole
time!"

The group turned and stared at Luis who smiled unperturbed, as if the story that had just been told was of someone else. Luis said he couldn't say for certain if there was truth to his friend's accounts, having not seen or heard anything strange in the house himself.

The newcomer, who we came to know as "El Brujo," the warlock, said that he too was skeptical, although he had also been born with a special gift, or perhaps it was a curse, he thought. He had the power to do that which others would believe impossible. He could call people back from the dead, make women fall hopelessly in love with him, despite their better judgment, and various other strange and wondrous feats. His revelation raised him to a level of supernatural ecstasy and he proposed a plan. He suggested we go back to the house and have a séance at midnight.

Since neither of us was eager to return to the dive hotel we were checked into, bombarded with acrobatic cockroaches, dingy walls and constant noise of twenty-four-hour traffic below on the avenue, we consented to go along.

i reminded myself of something my grandmother had revealed long ago. Spirits could do no physical harm to one; the only harm that could come would be from one's own fear. Hang in there, i told myself, for all i knew these guys could be doing no more than putting us on. We'd heard every other line used by men to get women to go off with them. It was feasible this was just an original approach.

It was almost ten o'clock, the hour when most people were accustomed to having their last meal of the day. On the way to the house, which was walking distance, we stopped and picked up beef tacos, garnished with green sauce, Cokes, and a bottle of rum. Luis ducked into a store and purchased a Ouija board.

It was a long trek to their house as we made our way like pilgrims. You and i were already exhausted beyond words. There is no easy way to describe the combination of fatigue, intolerable heat at a late hour in an unfamiliar city with intoxicated men who were for all intents and purposes complete strangers. Yet, our antennae went up and zoomed in on every move, each phrase to decipher whether foul play might be in store. This above all else, having to remain on guard because we were women travelers, persons with sparse funds and resources to count on certain conveniences and comforts, was draining.

As we walked, Luis, who kept at pace with me, told about the women who had stayed at the house during the summer. They had all remained platonic friends. His attitude was that if a woman was interested in a man, she would let him know. Otherwise, it was no big deal. This was the mode of thinking you and i had become used to with our male friends back home, but it was almost unheard of in this society. i wanted to believe Luis. He was young, attractive, intelligent. There was no reason for such a man to demean himself by being aggressive with women as so many we had encountered. Yet, we remained cautious.

Once we arrived at the house, which was clearly all it had been described, complete with three drafting tables in what was the dining area, Luis had his supper and went up to bed. He wished us a good night and a pleasant stay in the city.

Another man appeared. i don't recall if he was already in the house when we got there or had arrived shortly after. He was introduced to us also as a coworker and one who sometimes stayed in the house.

The brujo, in the meantime, seemed anxious to prepare for the séance. He asked me to join him in the kitchen. The lights were out and in the corner on the floor, he had arranged the Ouija board with two lit candles on each side.

"Before we begin," he told me with great ceremony, "we must call upon the spirit that will guide us through the séance. Is there someone you have been very close to that has passed on?" i thought of my grandmother and nodded.

We both concentrated, praying solemnly when the candles blew out. The brujo stared at me, for an instant i thought there was resentment in his eyes. "Your grandmother is here," he said between his teeth.

Coming out of the kitchen, he told us he would return precisely at midnight for the séance and left. i took a seat on the couch and noticed that the other man had put on the radio. Tropical music came over fuzzy air waves. He asked you to dance and you took his hand, quickly transformed from a lifeless mannequin to an animated woman, expertly following his steps with Caribbean fervor.

Ponce, the engineer who had thought we were from South America, took a seat next to me. Mixing a rum and Coke and taking out his cigarettes, he offered both and i accepted. A broad grin smeared across his face as he blatantly studied me. While with another man i would've been irritated immediately, i had the idea that this man was no fool and that we were about to enter a battle of wits.

He began, "I think you are a 'liberal woman.' Am I correct?" His expression meant to persuade me that it didn't matter what I replied. In the end he would win. He would systematically strip away all my pretexts, reservations and defenses, and end up in bed with me.

In that country, the term "liberated woman" meant something other than what we had strived for back in the United States. In this case it simply meant a woman who would sleep nondiscriminately with any man who came along. I inhaled deeply from the strong cigarette he had given me and released the smoke in the direction of his face which diminished the sarcastic expression.

"What you perceive as 'liberal' is my independence to choose what i do, with whom, and when. Moreover, it also means that i may choose *not* to do it, with anyone, ever."

The dark man winced. The crow's feet of his black eyes gathered momentarily. He hadn't expected that move by a long shot. He cleared his throat. Like an expert chess player, gave up a soldier graciously. "Really?" His voice cracked. "Well, you gave me that impression, you know . . . of being 'liberal' and frankly, you appeal to me. What do you say?"

Liberal: trash, whore, bitch.

The dance music creaked out of the transistor and you pulled away from your partner and went back to your seat, slumped down, closed your eyes. Your mind was distant, waiting, waiting with the enduring quality of a rebel slave.

The man you had been dancing with came over and said something to you and you got up to resume your dance. Instead of keeping up with the fast-paced rhythm he insisted on slow dancing, drawing you near his sweaty face and stale breath, to kiss your hair, whisper something inaudible in your ear. You pulled away, but kept dancing.

You reminded me of the tale of the little girl with the red shoes. Dancing did for you what drugs did for others, what cigarettes and alcohol did for me, created a transcendental ambience in which one could flow with the tide. When he pulled you close again, you resisted and went back to the chair.

i analyzed my challenger's face. He had just made a comment as to how well i kept up with his drinks and cigarettes. i knew it was meant as no compliment. i was used to that attitude and wouldn't allow it to inhibit the enjoyment of my vices.

He wasn't a bad-looking character. i was certain he had had

the experience of convincing many a good-hearted woman that he'd been the one she had waited for all her life. Afterward, she would go on waiting, for promises to be fulfilled, his return late at night, her child to bear his name. His persistence was impressive but not admirable.

"i have already told you," i said firmly. "You have obviously misinterpreted my being so-called 'liberal.'" We didn't talk for a while, busied ourselves with the drinks that turned lukewarm in the hot night, tapped cigarettes into the butt-filled ashtray.

You got up to dance again.

Ponce spoke up, as if no time had lapsed since my last comment. "Oh yeah?" This time he lost a knight, a bishop, perhaps his queen.

He poured more rum into my glass and dropped an icecube to stall for time, most likely to think of a comeback that wouldn't cause him to lose any more ground.

"Tell me then," he asked trying not to lose his self-assured smile, "when you meet a man, what kinds of things do you like to know about him?" We both stared at each other, eyeball to eyeball, then simultaneously reached for the pack of cigarettes. He took two out. Lit them and handed me one.

i answered frankly. "i am interested in his persona first, what his perspectives are in terms of his environment, his society, his government. In other words, whether or not he is a pig." He cocked an eyebrow, surprised that a woman would be interested in such issues but had the sense not to make light of it.

He told me of his background, his mother, who had been a prostitute in a whorehouse where he was born and raised. Until the age of ten he lived, worked and played in the red light district of the city. At that point, he ran away.

It was a priest who took him in and put him in a home for boys. He was encouraged to study, learn the basics. As he grew up, he thought seriously of becoming a priest, but went on to study at the university instead, and finally became an engineer.

i was glad to have a real conversation while still in the midst of decadence and absurdity, destitution drawing ever near, and a travelling companion who entertained homicidal thoughts. i didn't tell Ponce how i felt. A man who really wanted a woman sexually would undergo at least a few of the challenges set out for him. What was an hour of general discussion if it meant he'd have his way ultimately?

He took a sip from his Cuba Libre and turned the game over to me. He asked me my age. "Thirty-two," i lied. His expression showed he wasn't convinced. i had added about ten years to my life. "Why should i lie about my age?" i asked, feigning indignance. i was the one with the smirk.

The reasoning behind my contrived number was simple. It felt as if each of my years since i had left the nest had been equal to dog years: $6 \times 7 + 16 = 58$. Thirty-two actually became a conservative figure.

"Have you ever been married?"

"Yes, of course! Three times in fact, and three times widowed!" Suddenly i was gay. "Ah! The merry widow!" Ponce laughed and we clinked glasses. The irony of it all was that he seemed to have accepted what i told him, probably because it was scandalous.

You came back to sit unable to endure your dance partner's stubborn advances any longer. Ponce looked at you and asked for confirmation concerning my marriages. You nodded in a manner that i knew was born of indifference but to him was clearly matter of fact.

He seemed convinced. For good measure i added: "i am very bad luck, i suppose, at least to the men in my life." Ponce frowned and glanced at his watch as the front door opened and the brujo came in.

It was one minute to midnight. We watched the brujo as he went across the room in slow motion, his eyes, red, fluorescent beads and without a word, slumped into a chair. He took out a joint from his breast pocket and lit it. After taking a long drag, he passed out.

You and i stared at each other. It was time to be on our way.

Ponce didn't try to stop us and proved to be the perfect host. He walked us to the street where he hailed a cab; giving the driver a few bills, he wished us luck and said to come back if we found we needed a place to stay.

Checkmate.

Letter Twenty-Three

HOT WOMEN! *¡Caliente!* La crème de la crème
the vamp world in competition for the throne
banners across broad shaven chests representatives of
the Amerikas—ah yes! my friend, we were two schoolgirls
in comparison to
sizzling dynamite
silicone
hormone city
    Swiss made caricatures of the female genus
    and we, dull, lusterless next
    to statuesque illusion. Those men
that is, those in pants
did not care pinched a tush here nibbled a bare shoulder
Let's toast to the loveliness of the drag queen!
Dance, take him to a hotel sign the register without pomp and
pretense Mr. and Mr. Let us not be amused and ridicule him
but ourselves for he has created himself in his own image
narcissism without patronism—Behold the eternal flower!
while we go 'round and 'round in never ending hypocrisy
        At the table with a faltering
leg we watch the finalists quiver with anxious glee
for someone will win in this competition someone will reign.
Second runner up, first runner up, Ladies and Gentlemen:
our queen for a day, Miss Venezuela!!!
(No "Ms." here and no medical exams to assure
we have nothing but virtuous señoritas representing
the *patria*)   He accepts with lopsided tiara
on a blonde wig not without a modest display of gloat
and arrogance but wait—Miss Puerto Rico will have none
of this!
Someone was paid off! Something was rigged! Bam! A hard

fist of accusation to a glass jaw a crowd gathers wigs
fly gowns tear to shreds the glitter diminishes to surreal
macabre
Come on come on says the Bert Parks of Miss Amerika-in-Drag
let us be one big happy family and celebrate without petty jealousies (which belong to the vanity of the female gender after
all). Miss Brazil jumps on our table to samba followed by a
middle-aged fatman in a brown polyester suit
a desperate attempt to keep the table steady

                                                                        fails
beneath their weight both crash to the floor the man a tortoise
feet and hands wave in the air rocks on his back grotesquely
the queen collects himself and sashays away with exaggerated
indignance. Ah yes—and a smooth-talking, sauntering like the
palm in a sensuous night breeze Cuban comes to take Alicia
out to the floor his lover casts the evil eye of the Caribbean
and no scene such as this is complete without Eric the Rapist
who weaves ominously in and out of the crowd like the shadow
of your ill-fated destiny waiting calculating and waiting
                        ¡Policia! ¡Policia!
With a wink of an eye the dancehall is abandoned
parking lot deserted
black ocean swallows the fiesta in a roar of engines
smoking down the road we are racing again
to meet fate head on.
                              And i didn't understand, Alicia
how you danced with such carefree abandon
when an hour before you had escaped violation at the point
of a gun
danced because he liked you whispered some falsehood
in your burning ear while his lover whispered in the other
he'd slit your vagina
and i didn't understand how dance made you forget
intoxicated enveloped you in sweet delusion like a hit
of pure cocaine
                        Later, at the private university
                              For the spoiled prodigy
                              of the very rich
where Jesús, who attended on a scholarship, participated in a
boycott against hiked tuition

                                        an invitation to dance
in the auditorium
                        with bored men fed up with poker
                        who should have had to coerce you
twist your arm threaten your life
lead you bodily in had only to *ask* you to dance . . .
                                        Again, the self-appointed
guardian, i follow
                        knowing there is little in the end i can do. i
have a vagina too. With all the tender fat which makes me soft
like veal there are no muscles developed to protect you no
black belt with a reflex of a paralyzing kick to the neck or
groin no hidden blade in my hair no pistol in my bag to surprise them when they attack and they will attack because
they're bored and they've been *waiting* for you. Eric leads them
on to the stage where you whirl and twirl to mambo rhythms
on a cassette. i called from the front row you smiled in your
inebriated state from one man's arms to another's and waved
and i had only to wait like the faithful slave because i was no
longer your friend and felt betrayed by your ineptitude to
grasp that in the lion's den one doesn't play by one's own rules.
It happened quickly. They were anxious to have you, chew you
up, one would have the legs, the other a breast, devour and
throw your bones into the ocean, never to be heard of again.
Another stupid desperate gringa, foreign scum. It happened
quickly. One grabbed your arm, the other pulled at your waist
to drag you backstage. Without knowing i would do it, i flung
at them. LEAVE HER BE! SON OF A BITCH! trembling with rage,
LEAVE HER ALONE OR . . . The spell was broken. The legend
that you were for the taking, that followed you from one city
to where you had never been before but reputation and honor
decides whether she will live or die—sentenced you that night.
All you had sought in Babylonia was a good time at a man's ex-
pense; but a widowed mother and his inheritance wouldn't allow you that. No! You would've been a blemish to his name
and you had to be dealt with appropriately destroyed, obliter-
ated.
LEAVE HER ALONE YOU SON OF A GOD-DAMNED FATHERLESS BITCH
OR . . . they left, in pairs, jostling like fun-loving schoolboys
who'd just been slapped on the wrist for a childish prank. You

stared with blank eyes as i led you by the hand out into the stark white of another day and perhaps, you hated me too, i had lied and said i didn't understand.

LETTER TWENTY-FOUR

Alicia,

The other night sleep evaded me. In the darkness i was reflective when my thoughts were interrupted by a succession of footsteps.

i was alone. For a moment my heart pounded. My mind registered that an intruder lurked in the shadows. Then, as i realized the footsteps were in that very room, had just crossed directly in front of me and had gone right in the closet, my pulse settled.

It was only a visitor who had lost his way across time. There was no purpose in getting up to check the closet, to pick up a weapon, prepare for attack. There was no one to confront. My trespasser had passed through this ancient place where memory gravitates those who'd left without realizing they had also died.

It reminded me of a memory of our own, that stemmed from the invitation we'd accepted while in the City of Babylonia, where we escaped death more than once and where death itself paid us a visit serving as the final catalyst to send us on our way.

The engineers we met in the plaza had extended an open invitation to the two bohemian women travelers, with no strings attached. When we took them up on it, we were satisfactorily welcomed like old friends.

Ponce hastily made up a room while i fought off shudders recalling the night when we had first met and had come to that house to have a séance. We were told then that this bedroom suffered from unexplained levitation of its furnishings (which included sleeping persons). The bed in our room had been known to rise into midair and shake.

i kept my fears to myself, knowing doing otherwise would make me susceptible to being teased and would only further my preoccupation with peculiar phenomena.

The engineers took us to supper with them that evening. We were not the type of women they preferred to be seen with, in our faded dungarees, long hair caught carelessly back. Thus, they didn't sit at the same table with us. We were equally indifferent to their company and simply were relieved to know we had found a place to stay.

When we got back, the house was dark, taking on the ominous tone of strange houses in thriller plots. Perhaps it was only my excessive imagination working toward giving me a bad case of jittery nerves. The phone rang. It was for Ponce, a lady friend. He smiled mischievously and left for the evening "on business."

The brujo turned up presently. He was disconcerted because the Ouija board we bought the night of the proposed séance had repeatedly refused to answer him. i decided to test it out myself, and Luis joined in for the fun.

You sat on the couch nearby, halfheartedly worked on a sketch. Soon enough it would be time for bed. A day in Babylonia was much like spending a day on a roller coaster ride, or at top speed on a motorcycle at the edge of a narrow mountain road with one's eyes closed. By nightfall, beyond sheer exhaustion, every nerve in our bodies had been titillated to its limit, each muscle screwed and hardened. We could do no more than sleep and hope that strength would come in the refuge of dreams.

The Ouija board responded to Luis and me immediately, but the spirit that had come to guide it was undoubtedly making as much a mockery of us as we of it. It ridiculed our questions, riddled rather than replied straightforwardly. The Ouija board merely played with us, the brujo insisted, and he was certain it was because it didn't like his presence in particular.

Luis was disinterested in the game and like you, waited for the stirrings of sleep to overcome him so that he might go on to bed. His fingers were lithe on the plastic instrument that darted and circled around the large letters and numbers on the board.

The brujo requested a sure test. We would elicit information that neither Luis nor i knew, a name, that of the brujo's deceased mother. Obediently, we requested the name only the brujo and the spirit knew.

Instead of replying to our question, however, the three pair of eyeballs pinned intensely on the gadget beneath our fingers as it began to slowly spell out its message. *A . . . L . . . I . . . C . . . I . . . A . . . N . . . O . . . S . . . E . . .* a few maddening skating movements of nonsensical spelling and then its final word, *M . . . A . . . Ñ . . . A . . . N . . . A.* We stared at each other, mouths gaping, then at you on the couch who were still withdrawn from our activities, appearing half-bored, half-asleep. You looked up wondering about the sudden attention.

Alicia will not . . . tomorrow. Alicia will not (what?) tomorrow? The brujo interjected "leave" or "rise" to fill in the blank. Not destined to *rise*?

"I'm going to die all right," you said drily, getting up and making your way to the stairs, sarcasm cut your words, "of want of sleep. Good night!"

You went up. After receiving the message about you, i was anything but sleepy. Reluctantly, i followed, not interested in continuing in the company of such a strange sort as the brujo. Besides, our sticking together had become a habit born of preventative measures. One without the other was surely lost to any number of fates neither of us could imagine favorable.

From the landing the brujo's cackling reached us. "¡Que duerman con los diablitos! ¡Ja-ja-jajajajaja!" His wish was maliciously contrary to the typical one of "may you sleep with the little angels." Instead, he sent us off to bed with little devils. You waved your hand behind you as if shooing off a pesty fly and went to brush your teeth.

Seeing how you hadn't been affected in the least by the Ouija board's message i didn't want to set myself up for criticism by trying to discuss it with you and, yet, i knew i couldn't put my mind to rest. Nervous agitation had the adrenalin going and i began to rattle on about anything that came to my head, trying to keep it light, wanting so very much to forget about messages from the beyond, little devils, cackling, and shaking, rising beds.

Alicia, only you know why you were so detached from your surroundings and turning your back said, "I really hate to go to sleep on people when they're talking, but I'm very tired. Good night." i had no choice. i shut up and turned off the light.

i called for sleep, eyes tightly closed, as fingers moved me-
thodically to each bead of my rosary.

Later, at a distance, there was the ferocious sound of a tropical storm brewing. A flash of lightning lit the room and my eyes
opened. There were hushed stirrings in the house. Perhaps it
was Ponce returning. i fell back into the abyss of the dreamworld.

Furious rain poured outside on the patio, bathing the foliage
that adorned the building's façade. We had gone to bed in scant
clothing, the humidity of the night suffocated. Again, i was
stirred from my sleep. i felt you leave the bed. You went to close
the door to our room. We had deliberately locked it before going
to bed, the skeleton key was in the lock.

Except for the rain that pounded against the red shingled
roof all in the house was deafeningly still. Just as you reached the
bed, your body jerked with a start. A short gasp escaped from
your lips. *The door was opening again!*

You had just closed it, turned the skeleton key . . . yet, we
both watched as it deliberately pushed inward. You jumped back
into bed and my hands were moist as i reached out and clutched
you
overcome by a hair-raising fear and while i knew why *i* was
afraid, i wasn't sure what caused you to tremble as you did in my
arms.
i recalled my spiritual guardian's advice, my grandmother, who
had told me long ago: *only fear could harm one.*

                                                              i told you
to close your eyes, what you might see your logical mind could
not rationalize and it would cause you to weaken. *It* would gain
power from your very fear.

                              Clutching the crystal-beaded ro-
sary in my hands and winding it around your fingers against my
chest. i whispered with an exorcist's will in your ear . . . *Our Father
Who art in heaven* . . . You'd never been indoctrinated into an
institutionalized religion, never heard eerie folktales from the
old ones who lived in the Sierra Madre or near ancient ruins;
never feared God or Satan, but there you were, quivering spas-
modically in my arms. *Hallowed be Thy name* . . . Something like
footsteps, but not footsteps, because there was no body, no feet,
but a massive rolling of energy blacker than the darkness in the
room, entered. *Thy kingdom come* . . . Thunder resounded like
enormous gongs, tears were torn from the sky, the shutters blew

open, your entire body jerked while i held on tightly. *Thy will be done* . . . It stopped at our bedside, rumbling, wanting, calling silently, pulling at our mortality. *On earth as it is in heaven* . . . At last, it gave way, rolled back in the direction from which it came. *Give us this day our daily bread* . . . The rain slowed to an even pace. *and forgive us our trespasses* . . . The door closed, the lock turned. *as we forgive those who trespass against us* . . . We lay motionless, taut muscles gradually unwound. *Lead us not into temptation* . . . Although our hearts still made acrobatic leaps, we were soothed by the peace that accompanied the delicate rhythm of the rain.

"Are you all right?" i whispered as if we had just been in a violent accident or thrown about in the throes of catastrophe, a tornado or an earthquake, rather than having undergone a psychological experience that could've resulted from no more than our lively imaginations, except that you didn't have much of an imagination when it came to the supernatural.

"Can you talk?" i asked next. Somehow the question didn't seem ridiculous, for my own voice had diminished to a whisper, the rest surely having fallen into my gut. You nodded again. "Do you want to call Ponce?" i suggested. Ponce was the one we had come to trust, but as your voice wavered through the thick air, we were suddenly conscious of our state, like children who had just awakened from nightmares.

As we heard Ponce scramble toward our room, apparently thinking a prowler had broken in and was accosting us, we remembered we weren't dressed and scurried into our night clothes and you unlocked the door. Ponce had given himself no time to consider protocol and was in his boxer shorts when he burst into the room.

After realizing we were safe, he looked down at his appearance and apologized. We didn't hesitate with explanations but ran out past him and straight toward his room . . . the only one we had been told that had never been *visited*. There, we both made ourselves comfortable in his bed and within five minutes you were fast asleep. Such was my companion of then. i don't believe there could've been anything to keep you from sleep short of beating it out of you.

Ponce came in. He scooted down on the floor, against the wall, and offered me a cigarette. It was probably the wind, he tried to explain our bizarre experience with a practical conclusion.

We both knew it couldn't have been the wind that stirred at the bedside as a dark coagulation. He had had similar experiences. Although admitting it was a presence from another dimension, he had wanted to approach the phenomenon practically and would have liked to know what it wanted in that house. Perhaps then, it would go away.

My grandmother had told me that if a spirit appeared before me, i should ask it directly what it sought because there had to be something that wasn't letting it rest and would have to be resolved. i offered my unpracticed wisdom hoping Ponce might prove a braver person than i and confront whatever it was that lurked within those walls and had scared the wits out of me.

As soon as Ponce realized you had gone to sleep, he changed the subject, however, no longer interested in the welfare of the ghost. "Have you really been widowed three times?"

If i could have seen his face better but for the darkness, i would've seen a delinquent's grin. His fingers reached out and began to stroke the length of my body over the smooth fabric. i turned toward you. Alicia . . . asleep like a big kid.

"He is not a was. He is an is," i replied. "Dark like you, younger, with a long way to go in life, i guess."

We were both silent and i knew he felt my nostalgia. His hand stopped close to my breast and i held my breath.

"Why don't you come to the other room with me," an idea he hadn't given up since we met.

"Are you kidding?" i made a joke of it. "i'm not going back into that room again!" He gave out a long sigh and rose. His silhouette in boxer shorts reminded me of the flamingos in the gardens at Sergio's hacienda in Merida. "Well, just call me if you can't sleep," he said as he left.

but deliver us from evil.

Amen

LETTER TWENTY-FIVE

In the morning we headed straight for the bus depot to purchase two one way tickets to Mexico City. We preferred traveling at night, that way we would arrive at our destination with the new day. Our tickets were for the midnight departure.

It was a long walk to and from the station, the sun hostile against the backs of our necks. A city in the tropics like so many situated by the sea, famous for its beautiful beaches, yet, we wanted no part of it. We wanted neither to bask at its beaches, mambo on moonlit terraces, nor to people-watch at its outdoor cafes, only to be rid of Babylonia with its vestiges of doom with every encounter.

We returned to an empty house, a business day as in any metropolis, the engineers were out. We went up and peeled off our clothes, perspiration drenched our fatigued bodies and we took our second shower since morning. Afterward, we decided to take a siesta, knowing from past bus rides, that we would get little sleep during our ride back to Mexico City. Without so much as a word, we automatically took Ponce's room, detouring around the one that had been ours.

Beyond the physical discomfort of unbearable midday heat, i felt feverish. The previous night's event had left us in a more sullen mood than when we'd come to the house seeking refuge from the streets of Babylonia. Suffice to say, women traveling alone were vulnerable to harassment from all sorts, but what had sought us out, at our bedside the night before, was the limit. "Better to face ten live men than one dead one!" i'd heard say, but now i wondered if in fact that would be my choice.

In my restless, dreamless sleep, i tossed over damp sheets and when i awoke, late in the afternoon, i found you sitting up, eyes intent on me. They were vague, pained with discountenance over the slew of mishappenings, the constant affront to our beings. "I was wondering," you said, a voice as strained as the tight lines around your mouth, "what would've happened to me if you hadn't been there last night."

i had no answer for you, but stared at the sorrow that had long surfaced. i wanted to make light of it all, obliterate what couldn't be rationalized so that we might have the courage to continue. "i'm still wondering what happened while i *was* there!"

My own doubts concerning prayer and the existence of a supreme being hadn't permitted me to convince you at that moment that it had to have been whatever faith still remained within me that had saved you/us. i was, after all, only mortal. i couldn't endow myself with superhuman abilities like the brujo claimed. i couldn't tell you that the mass of energy that had come in search of human life had relented solely because i had imposed my will on it, that i, by some spontaneously acquired valor, had saved you.

Saved you again? Like the night when we escaped gang rape at that university auditorium or earlier that night, when searching for you, i drove up with Jesús to that pitched black lovers' hideaway at a pier and you jumped out of Eric's car where he threatened to take you at the point of a gun.

No, you resented me enough for having an edge on society's contradictions by admitting to their enforced power over us, and you didn't need to believe i also had an edge with something as irrational as ghosts, demons, and God Himself by virtue of my own admittance, while you, as with the hypocrisies imposed on women, vehemently refused to accept that we were indeed in no position to protest.

Women in the United States could rally around government buildings, flash placards at media cameras, write letters of complaint to their congressmen (or congresswomen if that were the case) but in the ancient land where villages still remained unchanged since the sixteenth century, two foreign women with more book knowledge than the average local official, wearing the faded blue jeans of the day, bandannas tied brusquely around their heads and casually dropping socialist terms in conversation stood, little chance of gaining favorable odds.

And yes, i did acknowledge forces of good and evil that could tear at the root of a human soul because it had been embedded in me with as much conviction since birth as the knowledge that food and water were required sustenance if one were to survive.

When dusk fell over the city, casting an ominous gloom in the house, we went downstairs, listless and uneasy with the time on our hands before we would leave for the depot.

Across the room, you sketched what your lips couldn't express, two faces, side by side, hysteria harbored in the pupils. i tried to write in my journal but it was useless.

As the house finally drained of natural light, a strange sensation got ahold of us and we went out. Down the street, we went into a small restaurant to grab a light supper. Afterward, reluctant to return to the house, we went into another restaurant and ordered yet another meal. The engineers had said they would be home late. We discussed catching a film to kill more time, but after the second meal, we were too stuffed to do anything more than return to the house and brave whatever might await.

Contrary to the dread we anticipated facing an empty house, we found it full of very real, breathing men, the engineers with coworkers, and their boss, a fat, boisterous man. They were having drinks celebrating Mexican independence on its eve.

The usual night rain, light, liquid fingers tapped on the roof, against the windows; the usual rum and Cokes were passed around, the usual suffocating humidity of the airless atmosphere caused human discomfort.

Señor Salazar, the boss, was as happy as a child on the morning of Three Kings' Day to see the arrival of the female gender and insisted that we join him in a toast to his blessed nation. You, a confirmed non-drinker, as well as non-smoker, flatly refused, not concealing your intolerance of the indulgences of others.

i, on the other hand, had never been able to resist the pleasures of libations and a good Marlboro, along with the company of those who felt likewise. The engineers, fearing you might have offended their patrón, tried to laugh off what was clearly your unsociable spirit.

The other woman, in any case, enjoyed a good drink and a cigarette, did she not? They couldn't disappoint their boss, laughing heartily at his humorless jokes, taking pains to please him however they might, made an offering of me.

As you had come to observe on many an occasion, one or two drinks wouldn't affect me, nor three or four. In fact, many an evening had thus far found me sitting up, emptying bottles of brandy or rum with hearty male company without the slightest change in character or physical disposition. Never did i forget that in that country, such a woman was dubiously regarded. Yet, my self-assurance and ability to maintain an active discussion caused doubts in any man who thought he might succeed eventually in "having his way with me."

Enough of that. The point is, i drank and you didn't.

For a short while, Sr. Salazar reigned among his subordinates bent on granting his every wish, but before i was to finish my second Cuba Libre he lost his throne to Sr. Montes who came in with his chauffeur. Sr. Montes, as we were informed, was the head of the engineering department of the entire state. For this man's approval, our pitiful hosts did all short of falling on their knees. He was somber and as huge as he might have appeared in their humble minds, so imposing that you and i excused ourselves to pack, finding him a complete bore.

Presently, Ponce and Luis came up to wish us well on our journey and to tell us that their bosses too, were on their way that night to Mexico City, having something to do with the Independence Day's festivities in the capital.

Ponce said, a sly grin played around his cheerful expression, that señores Salazar and Montes had offered to give us a ride, if we wanted to join them. It would after all, be much more comfortable and convenient than the bus, not to mention saving the fare that we would undoubtedly use later.

(Now, dear Alicia, i know you are cynically recalling that after all we two brave, but not always wise, heroines had been through, there was no way we should have contemplated one more risk, make one more dubious decision to reproach ourselves endlessly for later, entertain one final opportunity to bring our tender youth to a quick end. Years later, only hindsight causes us to look upon the engineers' proposition as ludicrous, but we are not those of then, and if anyone else happens to read this account and would like to give us the benefit of the doubt, i warn him/her not to put money on it.)

The chauffeur was sent immediately to return our bus tickets and the rest of us went to have a late supper at the Paroquia. After the two suppers we already had earlier that evening, we could hardly have had an appetite. When the others had all finished, it was Sr. Montes who took the bill, pulling out a hefty roll of currency. No one flinched to see the generous tip he flung on the table.

With a regal hand, he gestured gravely and we rose in unison.

His unquestioned authority was impressive, but to us, who had encountered more than one man capable of such arrogance, his feudalistic manner was only to be humored until we left the great city of Babylon behind.

We parted from our engineer friends with warm hugs. Everything would be fine, not to worry, they whispered in our ears with the bearing of doubtful allies who had just turned us over to the Romans for a few measly gold coins. We were aware that our safety was no longer in their hands but left to the huge men who waited in their respective places in the limousine with the chauffeur like a horse with blinders at the wheel.

"You sit here," the chauffeur directed me to take the seat behind the driver, next to Sr. Salazar, "and you sit there," he said to you, pointing to the seat behind me where Sr. Montes sat as stiff as his starched collar.

As we drove away from the amber lights of the city, the drizzling rain began to fall harder and the road ahead disappeared. At first, Sr. Salazar was preoccupied with giving the driver instructions, fearing an accident in the drenching downpour.

i anticipated something disagreeable had already been arranged for us. i regretted my casual willingness earlier to drink and smoke, became aware of the low cut blouse i wore, realized that we had been staying in a house full of single men. What else could these two conservative, middle-aged types deduce?

When Sr. Salazar was finally at ease with the chauffeur's handling of the limo he turned his full attention to me. "Are you cold, dear?" He asked as an excuse to put an arm around my shoulder. My negative reply was in vain. i shuddered at his touch and my mind raced desperately designing a way in which we might again save ourselves from what might likely ensue.

i studied the unsavory man in whose presence my own stupidity had placed me. He looked like he had been married longer than i had been on this earth. He probably had a daughter i might elicit sentimental memories of. Why was he behaving this way—peer pressure?

"Tell me about yourself," he smiled, eyes twinkling, gave me a squeeze. He offered a cigarette from the pack he had pulled out of his jacket with his free hand. i refused. My head worked double time and i decided to play a hunch, having so little to lose under the circumstances.

"Well, i'm a teacher, a professor of anthropology. My friend and i are on this trip because i've been studying the ruins. i was especially interested in Chichen Itza. We're just returning from the Yucatán."

i snuck a peek from the corners of my eyes. It was working. He hadn't liked to hear i traveled with a respectable objective rather than gallivanting aimlessly, sleeping freely with whomever i met, like a gypsy astray from her caravan.

"Well, tell me, what do you like to do for diversion? You like dancing, having a good time, eh?"

"Actually, i've never had much time for it," i persisted to dissuade him from believing anything the engineers might have said about us. We weren't his run of the mill liberal, hippy gringas. "i like reading very much, and writing poetry. i also like music. My favorite is Handel, but Wagner is very stimulating for studying. Wagner is my father's favorite. i suppose that's why i love his music. We have so much admiration for our parents, for those of the preceding generation. i feel we can learn so much from it. You remind me a little of my dear father, bless his heart. He's so anxious to hear of my discoveries on this trip!"

Lying through my teeth! By the disturbed expression Sr. Salazar had assumed while listening to my chatter, i knew i had discouraged him sufficiently to reconsider his original intentions.

i caught fragments of whispered conversation in the back and realized you too had begun to spin a fairy tale version of the debutante exploring the illustrious highlights of Mexico, although i doubted Sr. Montes had a conscience about wanting to take a young woman who could've been his daughter! i doubted Sr. Montes could father anything but lizards.

Hours later, and the rain had long passed our swift moving vehicle when we approached a city and were told we had just arrived at the state capital. The two men had to tend to last minute business before moving on, and we were driven to a modest hotel. No one had mentioned having to stay overnight anywhere and as we feebly got out of the car, we stared at each other in near panic.

"For *this* we saved *four* dollars on busfare?" you whispered desperately. The transference of pesos to dollars did make the savings of the bus tickets seem meager and us ridiculous for again putting ourselves in potential danger for the sake of hold-

ing on to the little cash we had left. It was just like you to point
out the irony of our follies.

"Don't worry, i'll think of something!" i tried to reassure us
both, although my mind's resources by then were exhausted.
Short of making a run for it, we had really led ourselves neatly
into a trap from which there was no graceful way to escape.

To our surprise and great relief, we didn't have to resort to
fugitive behavior, make a fast grab for our bags and waddle away
beneath their weight like madwomen down the barren avenue.

We were registered at the hotel and left to ourselves with
courteous good nights from the two big wheels. In a few hours,
we were told, the administration desk would ring us and we
would again be on our way to Mexico City.

We followed the old man in charge of the desk up to our
room as he struggled with our duffel bags, stuffed like sausages
after weeks of traveling, collecting souvenirs and books at every
stop.

As soon as we were left in the privacy of our room, you
turned to me, your face flushed from the realization that we had
actually gotten away from the clutches of our pinheaded companions without having to undergo physical battle.

"You would have been so proud of me, Tere!" You were short
of breath. "Montes wanted me to go to a hotel with him . . . and I
thought fast! I told him that he insulted me tremendously. I said
I had come from one of the oldest, revered families of Cuba,
(now residing in the United States) and that I was engaged to be
married. He was pretty doubtful of my story at first, saying that
he couldn't believe we had been staying in that house with those
guys and not sleeping with any of them.

"Then he asked about you, if you had slept with any of them.
I said, '¡Señor, por favor! Don't insult my friend that way! She is
from one of the most respected families in Mexico City and has
also had a very strict and proper upbringing!' So that, I guess he
was a little embarrassed and said that he hadn't really wanted me
to do anything in the hotel room, just to keep him company.

"He told me he could make me happy in the future, that he
has a lot of property and offered to 'keep me.' He could get a
house for me and who knows what else . . . ¡Qué jodienda, man!
I acted very indignant to all of it. So, he finally just backed off,
but then, when we pulled up to this place, I didn't know what to
think anymore!"

We sighed and embraced. Our thoughts had been synchronized. The closeness we had felt for each other had been heightened by our desire to survive during our travels that had been filled with unpredictable dilemmas. Our masquerade had to be taken one step further to secure an arrival at the capital unencumbered by further suggested seductions.

When the desk rang shortly after the sun had risen, we came down dressed in dungarees, turtle neck sweaters, tennis shoes, eyeglasses and our hair braided. Each carried a book to read on the way. We were the picture of the collegiate daughters whose loving parents would be waiting anxiously for their return at the end of the summer excursion.

¡Ai ya-ya!
¡Qué jodienda, man!

Letter Twenty-Six

Mexico City, revisited time and again
since childhood, over and again as a woman. i sometimes saw the ancient Tenochtitlán, home of my mother, grandmothers, and greatmother, as an embracing bosom, to welcome me back and rock my weary body and mind to sleep in its tumultuous, over populated, throbbing, ever pulsating heart.

We arrived that day, the fifteenth of September, in style. The limo drove around the main square that was decorated with red, green, and white streamers and lights.

Then we were shuffled out like excess cargo, placed into a cab and sent on our way . . . presumably to the open arms of the loving family, but the address we carried was to the apartment of the family of a friend, a family that had shown certain hospitality to the wayfaring women from the United States.

That evening we sat around the snowy black and white televi-

sion screen to watch the multitude of patriots gather in the plaza
to catch a glimpse of the president.

i thought of my mother, thousands of miles and a country
away. She must've been thinking of me too, fantasizing how i
would celebrate that night with my millionaire fiancé in the
Yucatán, how fate had been so much kinder to me in her country
than it had been to her, the irony that her prodigy could go to
her homeland and be readily received by those who shunned so
many of their own so that they left their beloved nation to find
refuge elsewhere.

Three evenings later, it became evident that you and i belonged no more in that family's home than anywhere else we had
stayed during our trip.

We had telegrammed back home for money, my last paycheck from the job in California, your savings in New York.
While we waited, another myth involving Mexican tradition dis-
sipated before our eyes. Mexican hospitality did indeed have its
limits that could border on hostility and total lack of social graces
practiced on those who seemed to be questionable worthwhile
guests.

We tried our best to make ourselves invisible in that home,
eating sparingly, sitting in corners. We had practiced the role of
the unwanted foreigners and continued it with disappointment
when we realized we weren't among friends.

A telegram arrived from the Yucatán. The lady of the house
handed it to me suspiciously, waited for me to open it, but already knowing its contents, i slipped it into my pocket and with
you, went to the bathroom to open it.

During the episode we had lived well in the Yucatán, with a
host who had promised me a new life free of hardship and
worry, you had expressed no enthusiasm. It had always been a
farce to you, an incredible fairy tale and after our experience in
Babylon, even a chapter to recall bitterly, rather than with whim-
sical memories.

i handed you the telegram. You opened it and began to read
aloud a melodramatic adieu of as much ingenuity as one within
the pages of a dimestore romance novel.

"My dearest Teresita, Ours can never be. I wish for you the
best . . ." My face was to the ceramic tiled wall. A chill ran
through my veins.

"Oh, Teresa, I'm sorry . . ." i heard you say at a distance. How could anyone ever apologize for another's not having won the grand lottery? You shouldn't have apologized for my vulnerable romanticism, but i suppose you felt compassion because you loved me as Sergio had not.

Coward! i uttered under my breath each day before i boarded the plane that brought me back to the city i had known most of my life. Coward! i spat with venom on delicate sheets of onion skin paper meant to be mailed to that paradise home in the peninsula, but were balled up and thrown in the trash instead.

Coward! i sobbed in private in my mother's home when she took one look at me having returned with no more than mosquito bites and tarnished skin brandishing my luxuriant days with a wealthy lover who had only taken to bed a liberated gringa.

"You were married, divorced, been around, a veteran of various wars . . . How could you have expected him to take you seriously? Men like that, with status, money, use women like you for playthings!" She never looked up from her sewing machine as her foot pressed hard on the pedal. Her words sowed themselves into my depleted spirit.

i left the white, handspun tablecloth with intricate embroidery and eight matching napkins, the pillow cases styled in Oaxacan tradition, the greenstone ring and the tiny gold cross on a fine chain, souvenirs all selected with special care, carried from bus depot to bus depot over a period of months, across thousands of miles back to place before my mother, tokens of my humble regrets that i couldn't have done more.

Pulling over my head a woolen poncho to keep the October bite away from my battle-fatigued body, i quietly closed the door to my mother's home behind me without saying good-bye.

Letter Twenty-Seven

Alicia,

i too suffer from dreams.

i haven't found a job. As the weeks pass, the poet and i stay up late into the night, the barren mornings find me in bed, pillow over my head to censor the quarrels of the frustrated lovers in the apartment below; my body weak from too much rum in too much coffee, and the constant ringing of the telephone at all hours when i am invariably the only one who answers it. The poet has many friends, and at times, it seems, he has none.

This morning i crawled back under the covers, after answering the phone for the poet who lay like a rock in his bed; and after drinking the entire jar of water we keep in the refrigerator, fell back into a dreamstate that carried me to a place that you and i have talked about often.

It was so vivid with detail i was certain i'd actually been there. The whole day i've been listless and my heart aches. i too suffer from dreams.

It was a provincial town, with cobblestone streets, shattered windows, and aged wooden doors and gates. In the scale of history: between the sixteenth century and the present. We found ourselves in similar towns during our excursions south.

The people were of mixed blood, people of the sun and earth. A late afternoon sun hit the thatched and tin roofs of adobe houses and cast long shadows along the narrow streets that wound and turned upward, then down again. It was a village where people had buried their dead for generations. Women in black clothing kneaded dough at dawn for the morning meal of their men. Children learned to read and write only until it was time to tend to the land: the land that was theirs, that had been worked to sustain their livelihood and very little more.

i too was of that small corner of the world. i was of that mixed blood, of fire and stone, timber and vine, a history passed down from mouth to mouth since the beginning of time when God, finding Himself lonely one eon of a day, decided to make a companion out of clay.

After shaping man after His own likeness, He set the clay to bake in the sun. When he returned to His model the following eon, it was pitch black. "No," He said, shaking His huge head, "this is overdone."

He shaped a second clayman and set it out in the sun to bake but this time returned almost immediately fearing the same result as with the first. This time, his prototype was pale, under-cooked and fell apart in His hands.

The third clayman He left out for the duration of one day, and in the evening when He returned, it was brown, firm, and strong. "Ah . . . !" He said, "I have at last made man!"

i walked alone through those streets with a sensation of pride and belonging. More than this: there was constant conviction that it would/could not be taken, at least not while i stood and breathed the fine mountain air and the rich harvest below.

i entered a house with a sense of familiarity, but it wasn't my house and i called to an old woman in the next room. When she came before me, i was surprised. This woman was not my moth-er. She told me that my mother was gone, but this woman was still of my people and we accepted each other readily. She of-fered a cup of coffee from an earthen pot.

On the sullen street i passed the group of young people caught up in rhetorical debate. They would fight and defend theirs with words and ideologies. They were fools, i scoffed, brushing briskly by them. i knew that they too, were scornful of me and my methods.

Then i met an adolescent who sat on the curb. He had been waiting for me. Although he recognized me, i only knew that he was needed. Fighting tears that were ready to explode from his eyes, his catharsis was one made of fears. At once i was his mother, comrade, friend, first love. Manhood had hardly touched the seraphic face.

It was likely that the night before us would be our last alive. i couldn't allow him to cower; there was so little time. He was to know manhood in its entirety in the next hour, witness the maca-bre of odious death and yet hadn't known the splendor of love and life even once.

Unbuttoning the faded print shirt i wore, he looked on with uncertainty and anxiousness. We stood in the middle of the street where the wooden and adobe structures on both sides could be touched at arms' length. i had difficulty with the shirt and while i struggled to be rid of it, the adolescent noticed the small girl who'd been following close behind me.

He wondered about her presence when we were about to make love, a child more innocent than even he. My reasoning was the same. The child couldn't be hurt by the sight of the natural act that had nourished the world with human life when she was about to see her own world destroyed . . .

We were interrupted. i swung around to a confrontation with the intellectuals who criticized my intentions. In rage, i tore open the worn shirt to reveal flesh. "i am a woman," i shouted, "but i am first human." i pushed them out of the way and hurried back to the house with the old woman.

Down the main road, on the outskirts of the village came the thundering sound of marching troops. They had arrived! i screamed to a cluster of rosary clinging women who trembled in a corner: "take the children! Find shelter! Hide!" Hurrying to a shelf piled with rags and feeling underneath, it was there. My weapon. It was my own and i had used it before, fit into my hand like that of a faithful lover.

i made certain that it was fully loaded and loaded another that had been left by someone else. *There was no time!* The moment had come and i was no longer concerned with the hypocritical accusations of the word dealers, the little girl who'd clung to my legs with silent vulnerability, the adolescent who would never grow up. The hour had come!

The hour that was for them, for us, for all who had awakened one morning to see their fields covered with blood rather than the harvest, who didn't seek to change the world but lived in good faith and prayer offered to an imposing God, for the young women who mended their mens' clothing and held their sons' mouths to the purple nipples of sweet breasts, for the man who watched the sun descend behind the mountain every evening and dreamed and when his sons were grown, passed on his dreams, for the black nights when guitars harmonized with the wind's song, to the bottle of regional brew, and a hand-rolled cigarette, to the baptism and a dance of celebration, to the aroma of soups simmering on wood-burning stoves and filled the bellies

of those who worked the fields, to a candle that burned in vigil
while a hungry mind gulped the printed truth of another's lega-
cy, to the owl that called from between the moon and earth while
lovers enwrapped their passion on silver tinted grass, to the
history of the world and to its future, to all that had lived and
died and had been born again in that moment as i approached
an opaque window and pointed my weapon.

                                                    Teresa

LETTER TWENTY-EIGHT

Alexis
is not his name
he has none
but a name is necessary
to call upon memory
of a blue flame
that sustained me
every hour
every day
every month
every second
every minute
every night
i breathed through him
my iron lung
Alexis
is only a name
and a name can be erased
unlike the memory

To have a woman love him for ever, a man need only keep
one or two of the milieu of promises he had made when it was

important to have her. Further, they must be promises that mean most to her. If he is such a dense idiot that he doesn't know which they are, then he deserves to lose her.

If he doesn't care and she persists being his, then she deserves to lose. The irony of it all is that in both cases, the two are losers.

Alexis Valladolid was not a flamenco guitarist, he was flamenco personified, your distant cousin who'd just come to the United States of America in search of fame and fortune, at the tail end of that year when we had been to Mexico together for the second time.

i flew out to spend New Year's Eve with you, knowing how the Rodney episode had left you. The woman he had been living with in your apartment while we were away, you found out, was going to have his baby. He hadn't turned away and shunned responsibility as he had done to you when you were seventeen.

All your paintings were muddled and purplish grey.

Alexis had crossed the ocean with his friend, El Gallo, and that entire week we were four, inseparable lovers, of life, art, music, and passion. Most of all, passion.

My first night with Alexis taught me that i was a virgin. i was a virgin and i had never given myself to a man before, nor had any man given himself to me.

High above the trash-ridden streets of Manhattan, the hornblowers, and double parkers, the winos, derelicts, pushers and pimps, the spicy aromas of cumin and garlic, curry, and fried plantains, burning tenements, stench of urined and vomited halls, blasting screech of subway trains, the winding and unwinding of life in all its naked forms, we were snuggled and safe within the tight arms of men who knew how to possess women.

Nights were twenty-four hours long and the mattress flung on your kitchen floor served as our marriage bed. i was pliable clay to be molded and defined, to envelop him, suit his proportions until a pillow was placed over the mouth to stifle a cry of insatiable hunger.

Behind the closed door to your room, time was measured by Argentine tangos and South American boleros on the record player. A bathroom door occasionally opened and closed quietly, not to disrupt a rhythm, bath water ran. Now and then someone went out for Chinese food or brought back fresh vegetables and eggs. The tea kettle whistled, cigarette smoke hazed the apartment's atmosphere.

You took a deep drag from a joint and stared at the watercolor tacked on the far wall, two phantom figures by the Atlantic seashore,
Rodney confessing lies, you, absorbing, enduring last blows of deception.

We danced. El Gallo admired your slender legs, remarked that they were like his estranged wife's, and thought you had her smile.

We drank cappuccino in Little Italy and ate cream pastries. We strolled through galleries in Soho, and Alexis whispered to you, "What does all this mean? Alicia—your work is better than this!"

We licked our wounds with the underside of penises and applied semen to our tender bellies and breasts like Tiger's balm.

One lethargic afternoon, we sat around, listening to Atahualpa Yupanqui and Víctor Jara on the stereo. El Gallo tended to the black beans on the stove. Your Christmas cards taped on the window by the kitchen table, languidly i read each one.

Alexis poured himself a cup of espresso, filtering the grounds through an actual sock since nothing else was available. "It's clean," you reassured after he gave a dubious look as you handed it to him for that purpose. You worked on a sketch in the corner of the room.

"*Wolfgang?*" i turned to you in disbelief holding his card in my hand. Was this the same Wolfgang whom we met in Oaxaca, who had left you with the bile taste in your mouth? You nodded.

"Who is Wolfgang?" Alexis wanted to know, eyebrow raised. You reached into the papers on the shelf and pulled out a neatly folded letter and handed it to me.

"He wrote you a letter?" i asked, almost in disbelief. He had given us no indication that he would be in touch, aside from taking a lock of my hair, it seemed that as far as he was concerned, nothing was to come of our chance meeting. i opened the letter carefully when a miniature photo spilled out.

Alexis picked it up, snatching it from my fingers in a brusque way. "He looks like a madman," he said sardonically. El Gallo came over and glanced over his shoulder. "He looks a little crazy, true. Maybe he is a genius, huh?"

i read the letter which was brief and filled with questions

about art schools in New York. Was he planning to come to the United States, i wondered.

"Who is this man?" Alexis addressed you. "A Nazi hiding out in Mexico?"

"Not hardly." You responded without looking up from your work.

"You can see the guy isn't German," El Gallo remarked, stirring his beans.

"He's Zapotec," you said finally.

"Even worse!" Alexis retorted.

"What do you mean?" i wanted to know.

"He's an Indian," Alexis said, as if the word made his meaning explicit. He held the picture, staring at the face as if it were of a criminal.

"The photograph is for you," you told me, still not looking up from your sketchpad. i read to the end of the letter. It indeed asked to deliver the photograph to me. Alexis handed it to me and lit a cigarette.

i sat on the floor at Alexis' feet, he at the table, looking at the small black and white portrait of what was virtually a stranger. Alexis, holding his cigarette between forefinger and thumb, obliged me a puff. Then i detected an odd scent. i drew the picture close to my nostrils. It was drenched with some putrid oil. The back was stained brown. My head whirled.

"Alicia . . . this picture . . . stinks . . ." i said, putting it down. My head began to tighten. Everyone took turns bringing it close to their noses and then looked oddly at me.

"It has a slight scent, Teresita, like oil or something," you repeated, "but it's very faint. I think the poor dude was trying to arouse your senses not make you throw up . . ."

Neither of the men could detect any scent whatsoever. i picked up the photograph again and instantly my head felt clamped. i thought i would vomit. i steadied myself and got up. Everyone wondered what happened as i went to lie down on the bed. My head throb wouldn't let me speak. i was overcome with sleep, sleep would make the throbbing go away, the clamps at each side of my head stop pressing in, threatening to crush my skull.

When i awoke, perhaps an hour or so later, but the days are short in winter so it was dark, i remembered, as if i had dreamed it, and called you.

You stuck your head in the room. "Feeling better? Hungry?"

i motioned to you to come in and close the door. i sat up. Whatever it was had passed. "Alicia, do you remember when you left me in Mexico City and i was waiting for my cable to purchase a flight back? The day i got it, i went to the bank immediately and then i got a ticket at the airline office.

"When i came out of the building, there was an old beggar right outside, his hand stretched out. My wallet was still in my hand and i couldn't help but give him some change. When i started to walk away from him, at first i thought he had said, 'gracias,' but then i realized he had said, 'no te vayas,' don't go. i turned around but he was gone. He was nowhere, Alicia. Maybe he disappeared in the crowd or went into the building . . ."

You stared at me, wondering why i had chosen that moment to share that story with you. Beggars were not an uncommon sight in Mexico and men would be men, even beggars. Why shouldn't he want a generous lady to stay, you asked.

i closed my eyes and saw the old man again. i remembered the photograph of Wolfgang, the same hair, jawline . . . the same sickening smell!

"Does that mean you don't want the photograph?" you wondered.

"That means you should burn it."

"Alexis already has," you told me and left the room.

LETTER TWENTY-NINE

As you may recall, in Chicago, i found refuge with a fellow poet. His drug addiction was romanticized in the grand manner of all maestros.

i'd returned from Mexico without a husband, without the entrepreneur from the Yucatán i had written home about, with only the faithful pair of dungarees and the many filled notebooks. i hadn't so much as a coat to stave off the winter or boots to shield my feet from the Midwestern snow. My family wanted no part of me.

The poet/roommate bore a star of luck above his head when it came to receiving money and was a generous friend. So we ate well when he received a royalty check or an allowance from home, which was most often the case. We drank happily into the night engulfed in our obsession for the written word, and being that he also smoked like a fiend, there were cigarettes.

We were the best of companions because we didn't compete in personal matters. That is, i deferred humbly to his talent and as he was homosexual, he wasn't interested in making me a conquest.

The poet couldn't have expected me to return with anyone from my brief visit to New York, but somehow, he readily understood. He knew the level of degradation i'd been subjected to, the rejection of my family, that the inability to find a job stripped my self-respect. He knew i needed someone's approval of my existence.

However, the first days after our arrival, he was resentful of Alexis' abrupt interference in the unorthodox pattern of our domestic life. But like you and me, was won over when the fringes of his poet's soul were set ablaze by the guitar of a man who loved no one and nothing but through his intense playing.

Alexis was able to enrapture the most insensitive of listeners; his mane of almost blue hair fell over the furrowed brow deep in concentration, a disarming, boyish smile afterward took everyone and made them his. At least that is what the poet and i agreed upon in all our verses that were dedicated to Alexis Valladolid.

P.S.

And i don't know how long we would've gone on, the three of us, an irregular triangle of spirit and lust for life, in anachronistic fusion.

Alexis loved to cook, but being ever the man among men, i was alone relegated the task of housecleaning, and the poet, of course, paid the bills. This is how everything that consisted of our lives, worked out. Alexis took the dominating role and designated ours depending on his mood.

This was not a man conflicted with mestizo blood and inferiority complexes of the evident sort, but one complete with a silver cross that hung from a rope around his neck against a hairless, sunless chest, and a knowledge of the other side of the story that neither the poet nor i had ever thought about.

His embraces were poison. His passion always painful. He professed sincere humanitarianism and took avid interest in our community undertakings. He became a grand companion of the poet as well.

Once i awoke without him near and found him rocking the poet to sleep like his own child, the poet's massive head grotesque as if decapitated, in my lover's arms. In the softest of voices, not meant to be heard a hair's breadth away, Alexis sang to him as he had never sung to me.

Then the fire of Alexis spread, not just throughout our souls that ached for understanding, protection, approval, but to our minds and it manifested in petty jealousies and competitions for his attention.

He preferred the intimacy with woman to that with a man and the poet deferred, leaving us his apartment to pursue our madness until it destroyed me, as the poet professed.

LETTER THIRTY

Este niño no tiene cuna
su papá es carpintero
él le hará una, El Gallo knew the gypsy lullaby and probably sang it to his children when he returned to Spain. After he was gone, there were several phone calls between us. We decided that it was best not to expect El Gallo to keep his word that he would come back to New York. Alexis, who had been his friend since childhood, agreed.

Pursue your work, morena! Alexis advised once, taking the telephone receiver from my hand, commanding that you put aside concerns of the sentimental nature and cast all else to the wind. Find gratification in your work! Alexis was a model of his own advice. Disciplined to a fanatical degree, loving a woman only as long as she was tolerant.

In autumn your portfolio was accepted at a prestigious school and you set forth to pursue a degree. (Who cares about degrees and institutions? Alexis scoffed. A degree is a good thing, i protested.)

Your parents' pressure in the end was the deciding factor. They didn't want to see their only child waste her life vagabonding, living the bohemian life past the "experimental state of rebellion."

As for men, there were a few, platonic friends, but when you decided to take direction with your artistic aspirations, extreme measures also had to be taken to secure your emotional stability.

A womens' group you joined kept a policy that all members had to remain celibate in order to achieve total self-sufficiency. For individual as well as joint independence, each member had to detach herself from any form of reliance on men.

In your sessions you discussed the reasons why, for each woman, celibacy had become necessary to the pursuit of her career. One may have told how she had been molested by an uncle as a child. Perhaps another shared the details of rape in the corridor of her apartment building, or had been awakened in the night to find a faceless man over her bed with a knife.

It is possible there were spiritual beliefs that insisted on abstention for those wanting to reach paradise and to see the face of God in the afterlife. Maybe, some just didn't like men.

You might've fit into any of these categories for all the alienation you now felt sexually toward men who before you had so much enjoyed, before Mexico, California, the final breakoff with Rodney, and, of course, before you'd realized that the existential Gallo had intended all along to go back to his wife across the ocean.

"You're biting your nose off to spite your face," i resorted to cliché since all else hadn't seemed to give you doubt regarding your new mode of life. It would only be for a while, you said, with a paper thin voice as if we spoke to each other from across the globe. In fact, it lasted a very brief while. But who counted the days?

You found a neat apartment walking distance from the school and lived off your trust fund with meticulous budgeting. You were at last, on your own, but it plagued you: the absence of what you couldn't pinpoint to anything but nature yielding your body and spirit despite society's obstacles. Men and women belonged together.

You craved a family, to share life with a steady man, and children to sit around the table together, hold fast to each other during winters, and to go out to play in better days, always as one unit.

Men and women were partners in the deepest sense. It wasn't the task of one or the other to be economically responsible or to tend to the raising of children.

Yes, yes! i agreed with you emphatically but it was a period in which all those ideals were twisted and made perverse by the man who held me rumpled, like composition sheets, in his tight grip. All my words you weighed with the awareness that i was by no means in a position to do what i believed.

You were on your own.

You shared your thoughts with a Viet Nam veteran in your animation class. He waited for you afterward, in the cafeteria, to have tea and yogurt. If it grew dark while you were engrossed in discussion, he walked you home.

He was impressed by your firm convictions, your courage to stand on your own, to be able to leave love and sex on the wayside because your work was easily as important as it could be to any man. He sought you out to unburden himself of his own torments, for your sound responses, the manner in which all matters were clear cut to you evoked his admiration.

Abdel, you told me, had vestiges of Caribbean blood, a man without a surname, born and raised in New York, a product of its streets, with an agitated manner that made one feel as if he was always thinking of something else rather than fully concentrating on the subject at hand, always ready to get up and leave for some crucial engagement, while not making a move for hours.

He was in the process of a difficult divorce. Before he had gone to Viet Nam, he had hopes of being a filmmaker, to perhaps direct documentaries. New York, after all, was loaded with material! His wife had held the family together while he was away and afterward, when he returned and suffered a nervous breakdown.

He continued to lapse into depression, had losses of memory, listlessness, and she filed for a divorce. He had no chance of getting custody of their children, and only hoped she would be sympathetic in court and allow him visitation privileges.

At the time, he earned only small sums of money here and there, doing free lance work. He wanted to move back to Manhattan, leave the brownstone to his wife and children, but because of the exorbitant rents, he would first have to find a roommate.

As it turned out, revealing more of his actual situation by the day, his wife couldn't stand to have him in the house anymore. She was angry and felt cheated by a life at home that had become hell. He didn't blame her, but felt her anger was misdirected. It hadn't been his choice to go into the army, much less to war, as a pacifist something he had adamantly opposed.

Why hadn't he just taken his family out of the country when he was called to duty, you inquired. And go where? He was flushed with exasperation as if the thought had already occurred to him many times before. He couldn't have pulled his wife up from her roots, where she had family, a career, friends. When would they have been able to come home? Maybe he should have retaliated, not allowed himself to be an inconsequential pawn for the government, but the fact remained. It was over and done with. It was time to start over.

It was time to start over, and the idea that that had anything to do with you didn't come to mind. By the end of autumn, you were roommates, and by the second night after he'd moved in, lovers.

LETTER THIRTY-ONE

Querida Alicia,

Forgive me for not having returned your call. i'm much better now and will be up and around soon to gather the pieces of the woman who was my self.

Sometimes we forget that lovemaking has another purpose and when i found myself pregnant, love for the man who had come to me like a shadow of the night seemed to have so little to do with my final decision.

My eyes were shut tight.

i felt the doctor's rubbered fingers intrude, probe for the size of the ignorant creature thriving within. i heard his metallic voice say to someone, "She's almost three months, it won't be easy for her. You'd better give her an extra sedative."

My palms sweat and brow moistened. Did the tiny body inside hear it too? Could it know what was about to become of it? Was *it* what wanted to let out a horrendous scream through my lungs, or was it my own terror stifled when i bit down on my lip to taste the acidity of a single drop of blood?

The assistant was kind, with water-filled eyes. My fingernails embedded into her sleeve. At a distance, she spoke soothingly, trying to divert my attention from the movements between my legs, the cold clamp that spread the vulva wide, the doctor's quick gestures that reached for unknown things. Something like a motor started up, and the most terrifying sensation my body has ever known began.

i erupted, a volcano of hot wine, soft membrane, tissue, undefined nerves, sightless eyes, a miniscule, pounding heart, sunless flesh, all sucked out in torn, mutilated pieces. How long does death take? My drugged head was heavy and oblivious to time.

"Please make him stop," it was my voice that pleaded, unintelligibly, but the sucking sensation went on, vacuuming organs, entrails, lungs. i couldn't scream, but moved my mouth like a gaping fish out of water.

"Only a little longer," i heard the maternal voice of the assistant come through the fog. Her white hands clutched my dark ones.

No, no . . . stop now! i wanted to say but couldn't, the affront would have to continue to its end. i repeated to my conscience that its spirit was unharmed and free to go wherever unborn things go . . .

That night, i rested in bed when the soft rap came at the door, a day too late. While at first he unsteadied me with his unexpected presence, i allowed him into my apartment.

His animal eyes stared down at me, the eyes of prey, no longer those of a hunter, but of a wounded buck, a fox caught in a trap, they pinned me further into blood stained sheets.

Slowly he came around. i recoiled to see him kneel before me. He bent his head and began to sob quietly. You can imagine the torment i felt hearing him beg for forgiveness and say he had decided he wanted to be a father after all.

i pitied him. The same pity i'd felt earlier for the creature spat out of my womb welled up again and i pitied the man before me with his arrogance. i pitied him because i thought it was love.

i had sent our child away, i told him, to wait out its turn to take part in this miserable world, where once being born it would no longer be innocent, for being was to survive and to survive, one must hurt weaker beings. No, the end of harming another living being was not the destruction but the saving of oneself, which becomes the true objective.

At last the meaning of my words penetrated his skull, and at that instant, those bestial eyes went dry to stare at me with disbelief or repugnance, which, i wasn't sure, or whether they were mirrors to my own eyes for i couldn't look at him, but waited for him to speak.

"You bitch!" His mouth foamed. Jumping to his feet, he raised his fists. Without the strength to lift myself from the bed, i dodged his hand. "You never think of anything but yourself!" Tears burned down his face.

"Do you think that while i lay on that table, having life sucked out from between my legs, i thought of myself? You come here drunk, as if this is your home, expecting me to cook, make love, when the only thing i want to do is vomit with disgust . . . !" i sat up.

"You, who talked about how much you wanted to have a child, how we would give it whatever it needed, even if we were poor, because of all the damn love we had for each other! Where was that fucking love today, motherfucker? GET OUT OF MY HOUSE!"

He didn't leave, not yet. He wasn't going to leave when i wanted him to go. That night he lay down next to me and we cried ourselves to sleep.

It was three days later, when he came in, returning my car, paycheck in his pocket, when i was up and about, able to cook, do his laundry, that he decided to leave.

He would cash his check and go drink with his friends. The next morning he would return to his studio. He had a chance to audition for a flamenco troupe passing through town. If he got the job, he would go with them on tour.

My head hung. He had stayed long enough to secure my tolerance.

"But, i . . . killed . . . my . . . baby . . ." i uttered, a sickening voice a thousand miles away repeated, i killed my baby, dully, like a lead club against an already cracked skull.

"You bitch," he slammed the door behind him.

It was a sun-filled, autumn afternoon. i remember because the concrete against my bare feet was warm as i wandered on the street, my childlike heart in search of a mother's consolation. The closest person to fulfill that need was my sister. i met up with her husband who put me in his car as i repeated, "i killed my baby."

"It's okay," he said. "We'll get your sister."

You know, she hadn't wanted me to have the abortion. She'd refused to lend me the money. The night before i went to the clinic, she cradled me and begged for me not to do it. "Forget that asshole," she said, with a mother's tears.

i knew she meant well, but i also knew he would never have been out of my life if i'd had his child. i wanted to be rid of him like a cancerous tumor. What would i have done with his child?

i am better now, my querida Alicia. i had to tell you this

because i owed you an explanation for my distance, because i trust you, and i know, no matter what, you have believed in me.

Always,

Teresa

LETTER THIRTY-TWO

A—

Love? In the classic sense, it describes in one syllable all the humiliation that one is born to and pressed upon to surrender to a man.

In Arabia still, a ritual is performed by which the clitoris of a small girl is slashed off to prevent her from giving in to some temptation that will dishonor her family. In India today, a bride whose dowry is modest, may be doused with gasoline and set ablaze by her mother-in-law so that the son is free to marry a woman from a more prosperous family. It is reported to the authorities as an unfortunate kitchen accident and the case is closed.

In no manner could i excel him. Even in the realm of household chores, i was permitted to do them because he had more important things to do, not because i did it better. My beans were too salty, the meat too tough. The plants not watered enough or over-watered.

My idea was fair but his elaboration of it made it worthwhile. He was the artist, i, a useless poet. i would do better giving up writing compilations of words. If i proved articulate, it was due to a college education, which did not necessarily mean i was intelligent. In one or two syllable words, he could make his point well enough to shut me up. Shut me up.

My sole endowment was that which is uniquely female and widens a man's nostrils with its alluring scent. Until i succeeded in boring him with my persistence to remind him of commitments, *that*, at least kept his interest.

A woman takes care of the man she has made her life with, cleans, cooks, washes his underwear, does as if he were her only child, as if he had come from her womb. In exchange, he may pay her bills, he may not. He may give her acceptance into society by replacing her father's name with his, or he may choose to not. He may make her feel like a woman, or rather, how she has been told a woman feels with a man—or he may not.

He may be so magnetic that other women readily give up all to take him to their beds. They don't know he may beat his woman when he's drunk, that he reproaches her for not being a good childbearer, tells her she is plain and no one can stand being around her because she is so pathetic.

She may have a clue that he has found someone else to capture his interest. She now looks like the shadow of the new woman who radiates with his passionate attention.

There isn't a woman who doesn't understand this deathtrap. You understand, Alicia, although you never talk about it.

After a while, she adapts to neglecting herself more than he can. Her nails are bitten to the quick. She forgets to eat or eats when she's not hungry. Her inability to sleep makes her face droop like the jowls of an old hound dog. She is twenty-six years old.

With nervous gestures, she tears an invisible thread from the edge of her slip. If she doesn't watch out, she will quietly go mad and no one will have noticed.

Then one October night, she has finished a fifth of rum alone and dares to take out the poems she wrote in another life, before him. The voice of a woman who rebelled—who stood like a marble statue of Athena, who swatted at men's pretentious attempts to control her, like swatting a gnat or a malaria carrying mosquito, with caution but with confidence—calls to her with muffled shouts.

She begins the methodic process of gathering the pieces of that woman, like the jagged pieces of a broken china vase, and glues them together, patiently, as neatly as she is able.

She must find a job. There are visits to the psychologist at the free clinic (whose eyes she can't look into because they are the enemy's eyes), the blank notebooks to fill.

A new woman friend brings food from her pantry because this one's dinner has been a cigarette, a hard-boiled egg, and a cup of instant coffee every night that week.

She frames a drawing she made once when he had stayed out all night. It is of a woman whose eyes bulge comically and whose hair is aflame, but who sits with hands restrained on her lap. She wears a *rebozo*, her traditional shawl, and the face is her own Indian one.

She makes decisions, takes her life back into her own hands. If loving a man, loving men who run cities, states, countries, establish organizations, head schools, manage and own businesses is surrendering oneself to a level of inferiority simply because—

No! i lied . . . Oh, Alicia, if i were back in that miserable hotel in the ancient city where gods, warriors, and women all fell beneath the blows of imposing invaders but what killed them was their disparate energies, i wouldn't deny to you again that i understand why you hated yourself.

You weren't the desirable, soft, uncomplicated, maternal/child, buxom, ever-enduring lap and embrace, blonde, vivacious, cherry red puckered-lipped, plastic starlet of Hollywood movies, the saintly madonna, any image, illusion, delusion, hallucination, glossy, celluloid reproduction, stereotype, cliched man's definition of what a woman is and has to be. Therefore, you would not be *loved*.

Sometimes, you settled for basic copulation to attain a semblance of human warmth, in lieu of compassion.

You had been angry that i never had problems attracting men. You pointed out the obvious, the big breasts, full hips and thighs, the kewpie doll mouth. Underlining the superficial attraction men felt toward me is what you did not recognize. i was docile.

T.

LETTER THIRTY-THREE

Alicia,

i had a dream of you this morning and the way dreams go, it was a collage of imaginary realities so that i don't know what to make of it. i remember how you appeared in that dream and that disturbs me. You were recoiled, drawn into yourself and pathetic. It isn't the image of you that i have now, but since i've had no word from you for a while . . .

There is an epilogue to a certain chapter of my past and i hope to amuse you with the telling of it, because i am very pleased with how it ends.

i saw Alexis again.

It wasn't a big coincidence, being that we were both at the nightclub he always frequents and where i've read in the paper he plays on Wednesday nights, and maybe i thought i would see him but that is not why
i went. It was to see a wonderful group that was in town making an exclusive appearance. i said to myself: what the hell. i've got to go to this concert.

Well, i was in fine form that evening, you understand. i'd spent the entire afternoon at the beauty parlor having my hair restyled. i'd dined at a superb nouveau cuisine restaurant, danced at a club with a new interest, who, with the champagne and his wonderful sense of humor, made me forget the slightest preoccupation i might have had with life.

All this time the plan to go to see that group had not been made, but when it was
feeling at the top of Mount Everest and nothing too great for me to conquer, we all jumped into a cab and went right over, walking into the dark nightclub with the show already underway.

They were fantastic, i have to tell you, four Jamaican angels calling to the heavens with their electric voices that sent currents through my body. When i saw Alexis at the table immediately next to where i stood, i think i laughed a little under my breath.

As i said, it couldn't have been a coincidence all the years i had avoided that nightclub like a hangout for lepers because i knew he went there.

His profile was to me, and it was plain he was with a woman.

i took out a cigarette from my clutch bag and from behind, tapped him on the shoulder. Alicia—the look on his face when he turned to give the light i'd asked for was worth its weight in silver pesetas. i took the light without thanking him and retreated into the darkness.

Epilogue

It was *her.*
The silence broken
after five years
the vow founded on
vengeance like fists
against the stained glass
windows of a cathedral and
she was beautiful. She has
always been beautiful her silence
stubborn will make her more
desirable still. What was it
to light her cigarette after so
many years? Afterward, I turned
back to the music that suddenly came
from another place, everything was past
pale and distant. *She*
was there, in the same room, at arm's
length. I had only to rise to speak
with her touch her cheek place my mouth
full on hers in the smoke-filled room
ask if she was happy if life had been better
to her than I if this moment meant that all
had been erased and we might start again
to see her head's imprint on my pillow in
the morning her attentive ear to my
guitar, smell the thick aroma of her
coffee late at night, and the deep

gutteral sound of her cries as
I loved her.
How does one get lost in a city? I'd preferred
the tales that she had fled but it was to
others she had gone not to another place
another continent another world and I had
sent her away all the while wanting
her
but a man doesn't plead he doesn't ask
he does not apologize. So I gave her
the light—all that she had asked for
in five years and from the momentary
glow of the match her lips were full
the bellies of birds taking flight.
She exhaled deeply.
The ever so slight curve of a smile
a mocking grin.
A man does not ask for forgiveness.
It is ironic that we should meet again
tonight while another female I've been after
so long is finally with me. (She is you
ten years ago, you know)
You
of innocent yearning without
question. You trembling with
fear of my will. You whom I kept
from your husband
home
family
friends
and made you only mine
a stuffed souvenir on the mantle.
Are you happy?
Did your relentless reproach give
you consolation? It is ironic
that we should meet again tonight
when it is this new one I prefer
a soft bosom to cradle my head
having rocked but one or two lovers
before me. Would making love once
more give your throbbing a rest? Forget

the sixteen-year-old bride I took when
you bolted your door unable to accept
the women I loved tho' never as much as
you? or the one I could not forget whose
portrait hung over our bed? Are you
happy?
You are as beautiful as you have always been
although tonight
you are different the hair
manicured nails the painted lips
and your new friends
waiting.
Your small hands limp bones such
a fragile being playing tough and
unfeeling.
I know you.
I will always have your love wrapped
in a winter night's desire when you belonged
to another man
a phantom at dawn
planting a kiss on each eyelid
believing I slept when you left.

LETTER THIRTY-FOUR

Alicia,

Finally settled back to the even pace of my quiet life after
having been caught up in the swirl of that eclectic city of yours.

Although i was proud to share the excitement of your first
one woman show it was too bad we never got a chance to talk. i
didn't even get to tell you my thoughts on the new work
that has that hazy, dreamlike quality of those early watercolors,

but heightened and given breadth with mixed media. If its intent was to provoke a disturbing response, you got it.

i refer, of course, to the series entitled: *La casita*. The figures in your series are angry dolls made of papier-mâché with hair from your own head. They stand at the dock with disproportionate dimensions and wait; black eyes stare at the viewer haunted by loathesome trickery. Their arms hang inanimately at their sides.

One angry doll inside the house, before a lopsided table with real, miniature copper utensils and clay vessels. The other drowns in the ocean, visible from the window of the little house.

The series goes on this way, variations of the memory in surreal honesty. The show seems to have been an enormous success.

i moved from one frame to the next without flinching an eye, conscious of the nervous twitch at the corner of my mouth. There were no tears. They dried with the remains of the fetus that had ended far away from oceans, casitas, dreams and follies of gringas and suave Latin lovers. It's past. The exorcism of the artist's rite serves only as a reminder.

What an angry doll i was to you when we first met across the dining room table in that house in Mexico. You laughed when i believed i would be placed in the little house and be cared for, although you didn't laugh aloud.

i don't blame you anymore that we were almost killed because you too had trouble seeing the world as it is. i think i was better at the masquerade although now and then i was caught up in it.

Our miserable experience across the land of beauty and profound intrigue didn't end with that horrendous night.

There was the telegram from the entrepreneur. i asked you to read it aloud, although i already had its message memorized at least a century before:

My Dearest, It saddens me more than you will
ever know that ours can never be . . .

There was your last night in Mexico when you didn't come in until dawn and then, it was only for your things. The lady of the house had locked you out. When i got up she ranted about your promiscuous behavior and how it had stained the morality of her household.

There is the vague memory of a man named Jesús who declared his eternal love one afternoon on a secluded beach. He abandoned us that night in an apartment full of sailors. He left saying, "This is my girlfriend. No one better lay a hand on her . . ." We went to sleep on the floor where tarantulas crawled and sailors snored.

i think of you, and you seem so far away. i hardly dream of you. Does this mean we're no longer the friends we were—or the same women?

My son is sleeping, his black lashes, flushed cheeks, the two fingers in a half-opened mouth fascinate me to no end.

There's something i have yet to tell you, Alicia. We're going home, Vittorio and i. Are you surprised?

In Cuernavaca, Vittorio's grandfather will take naps with him in the garden on the hammock tied to two tamarind trees. He will tell him stories he never told me. Mami will call him "hijo," rolling a warm tortilla sprinkled with salt and wrapping his little fingers around it.

My husband will be gone for hours on end. i'll read over students' assignments, eyeglasses hooked on the nose, feet propped up to pamper legs that threaten an outburst of varicose veins.

God bless and keep you, Alicia. i hope your upcoming trip to Europe will lead you to a place you'll want to go back to and call home too.

Always,

Tere

LETTER THIRTY-FIVE

Oh Alicia,

Even while i dreamed, you had stopped waiting for knights in shining armor, hoping of cradling little princes and princesses, whispering the lullabys your grandmothers once sang to you. There would be no babes to caress and coo, none to worry and fuss over, no bittersweet reflections in your twilight years of how they had grown up so quickly and gone off on their own.

i watched a special report on public television the other evening on China's policy on population control. According to the report, if the country doesn't receive full cooperation, the Chinese people will begin to starve in ten years. Married couples are allowed to have no more than one child. The question was posed at the end of the program, how would this country handle the problem?

Then i thought of so many adolescent mothers and i remembered you.

You were seventeen and, at first, had wanted the child, romanticized motherhood, life with its father, struggling together, the way young people do. When Rodney stopped coming around, you were afraid to be exiled alone.

A friend of a friend lent you her welfare card. The fee for a legal abortion was steep for a teenage girl with no one to trust who had that kind of money. At the clinic, you were alone, posing as a Puerto Rican woman who had already borne five children.

The nurse looked up the records and shook her head disgusted by your supposed negligence. She drew up forms that were not presented to you until you were on the table, sedated, feet in stirrups and exposed to the world the way you had never been exposed before in your life.

You were sterilized.

Maybe that Puerto Rican woman with all those fatherless children went on to have yet another child. Who knows?

Last month, at the opening of your show, which was meant to be a special occasion, with all your friends, your new lover, parents so proud that your strangeness had at last manifested itself in genius, i absorbed each work, a personal statement of violation and fear.

There were traces of Frida Kahlo and postmortem praise, her exposed heart as a blood pumping organ rather than the romantic metaphor expressing emotional rejection; and men, who are immortalized by women far beyond the limitations of their presumed greatness.

Love,

T.

LETTER THIRTY-SIX

When we
were twenty-seven, we saw each
other twice, both occasions indirectly associated with a member of the opposite sex. We were experts at exchanging empathy for heart-rending confusion known only to lovers, but you and i had never been lovers.

It is true we slept together curled up on the double seat of a rickety Mexican bus that wound its way through the nocturnal roads from one strange place to another; a soft shoulder served as a pillow for the other's head. A sleeping bag on foreign ground made us into siamese tamales. Like delicate creatures of an alien world we balled up immersed in networks of dreams, a foot spasm kicked the other awake for a

half-conscious moment.   It is true
we bathed together
                        in the most casual sense, scrubbed each other's
back, combed out one another's wet hair, braided it with more
care than grandmothers who invariably catch it on broken tooth
combs. We pierced each other's ears.

For the first half of the decade we were an objective one, a
single entity, nondiscriminate of the other's being. It wasn't
limited to hikes through scented woods, listening to passionate
folk music, the tranquility of reading aloud from passages that
drew meaning into our linear lives; not solely bound by the
synchronization of tai chi when in the midst of chaos we began
cranelike movements in slow motion one and its mirror.

It was natural that when my two week vacation came up, i
went to see you. i believed i was in control at last of the inner
centrifuge of emotions and wanted more than anything to   ·
                                    abandon
myself to laughter
as never before, not even as a child. Enough of the deprivation—
the faded underwear, neglected skin and hair, second-hand
sweaters, to not being able to attend concerts or a new film and
found friends happy to see me when we tangoed across a loft,
toasted to Piaf, told dirty stories and were children playing
grownups or imps mocking humans.

A modest income from my community job aided me in set-
ting out on this course. At the local drugstore, i purchased inex-
pensive lotions, cologne, lacquer for finger and toenails. i
brought out bright, embroidered Oaxacan costumes from stor-
age, picked up vintage clothing from thrift shops.

When the annihilation of winter passed, i was renewed. This
vitality, i took to New York to share like the discoverer of Cuauh-
témoc's hidden treasure to throw on the laminated top that
served as a kitchen table over the bathtub in your place. A pair of
lucky sixes, "C'mon, Mama, baby needs a new pair of shoes."

We were going to sit in outdoor cafes as famous artists had
done in days past, shop for a scarf or an antique brooch. i had
driven sixteen and a half hours just to ask you to *dance* with me—
but what i found was the carrion of what vultures in Mexico had
discarded. It existed in the five floor walkup, dusty refuge, and
moved only when it was expected to turn in a school assignment
or to get something out of the refrigerator.

The man
who lived with you was like a mean draft to one in the last phases
of pneumonia. He spent the food allowance on smoke and beer.
He brought unsavory types to hang out in the apartment. The
plants withered. The faded linoleum was gritty, dirty laundry
piled behind furniture, and you didn't want to come out to play.

LETTER THIRTY-SEVEN

Licha,

We haven't spoken to each other in months. Months? Months
would be nothing extraordinary, but a year is something else. It's
been a year that has passed between us like the silence of prisms.
i received only one letter for the three sent last year. You should
have been the poet, writing the letters you do, where one has to
decipher the images into a concrete message . . .
i gather you are well?

What's new with me? Not much, save the trip taken this
spring when footsteps were retraced to white sands of utopic
beaches. Yes, something of us remained, solidified by the potent
sun and engraved with the memory of travelers.

In the congested streets of downtown Mérida, circling and
winding in and out of little shops in hopes of finding the Mayan
costume at the right price, i found myself in front of the store we
knew, where the salesclerk and owner were familiar. Yes, i went
in.

i didn't dare let on that i'd been there before, that i was the
one of years before who had been courted by such a well-known
personage, friend of the shopowner, and was jilted flatly.

No surprise to any of his friends, i'm sure. i wonder if that was
why the owner didn't put the past behind us so as to give a
friendly reception, ask after my companion, the quiet Ameri-
cana with the long legs?

As it would happen, i drove past the hacienda. Glancing at that instant, from the corner of my eye, i saw him. It was the end of an ordinary day, hot like so many since then. He could never have imagined in that VW that had just sped by, a ghost took a mental snapshot, made a portrait of the memory.

You may wonder why, of all places to vacation, i chose that one. It wouldn't let me rest. In all honesty, the men, the bitter resignation, hold no significance and didn't hinder the beauty of the place.

There are recollections everywhere we turn, the cafe down the blvd., the movie house on Clark St., mutual friends. Why hold a grudge against a place, a country?

When you were in Rome, an Italian, who had stayed with you for six months, slipped out of his loafers one day and went out through your balcony and never came back. Should you resent Italy? Should you burn the loafers?

In Cuba, when you were left to sit out an entire evening because your lover had set out to dance with every blond in the club—did you condemn the entire revolution?

i want to take my ghosts, Alicia, confront them face to face, snarl at them, stick out my tongue, wiggle my fingers from the sides of my head, nya-nya!

Maybe we can plan a visit, a visit to make a new plan. i don't want to ramble, i want to talk with you again.

                                                                    T.

LETTER THIRTY-EIGHT

It is no longer a secret.

The poet, whom i hadn't seen in years, was making his rounds throughout the Americas when he ran into you and Vicente das Mortes in Puerto Rico.

How long did you think i would tolerate your growing pains?

Before i left Manhattan, wanting so much to have you come out and dance with me, rid yourself one night of memories and heartaches; such a young woman to be so sad forever, forget the man who inhabited your apartment and would leave it without so much as a "thank you, ma'am," i'd told Vicente about you.

i left out the banal details and put all that was wonderful about you in a small velvet bag like a magic charm so that finally he insisted that you join us.

You danced all night with his cousin, Egberto, who held your nimble body taut through merengues and guaguancos. The tortoise combs in your long hair that was flaunted in the faces of the other dancers, gave the illusion of innocence. The ivory, satin dress with Cinderella sleeves, enhanced it so that Vicente, watching from our table, believed you might
love him.

i knew this when he said he would like you to teach him to dance. i smiled enigmatically, certain that soon, he'd realize you weren't a child, a mother, a vessel that poured forth. Teach him to dance? Of course i wouldn't mind! "Ah! Minha Dulcinea!" He smiled as he kissed my hand.

You would find it in yourself, search way down in your generous soul to teach this fine, buck-eyed South American to dance like the folks on 42nd, like God meant for people to dance when their spirits and troubled minds gave way to the movements of the limbs, feet and torsos and when the rhythms of drums, gourds and wooden flutes sounded.

What else did you have to give Vicente das Mortes but dance?

The poet was "clean" when he passed through here on the way to Machu Picchu. He had outwitted the beast of heroin.

We talked for a long while, drinking espresso, hearing him tell of his adventures through poems. He walked me back to my apartment when he remembered the pale woman with the tortoise combs in her hair, my old compañera. He remembered the picture by my typewriter, both of us in Villa Hermosa, with the huge Olmec head in between.

He had seen her dancing in San Juan and someone had introduced her and the Brazilian boyfriend. Apparently they'd been living together for some time in Río Piedras. He hadn't caught your boyfriend's name but recalled that he whispered, "Dulcinea" all evening, and each time, you had a smile that oozed with honey at its sound.

LETTER THIRTY-NINE

Last winter i felt an urgent need to get away.

Being inclined to be surrounded by a few friends, i needed to go to someone familiar, who didn't make me feel alone. You had your fill with Abdel. So my long lost husband had to do.

It wasn't out of desperation that i proposed a visit to him. Since our separation i've seen him only once before but that cat gut string that binds those who've endured hardships together and shared good times has kept us close.

His initial reluctance to have me come for a week didn't discourage me either. i understood his reservations had to do with the confrontation of my role no longer as his wife. He relented in the end, and i took the earliest flight to L.A.

He was dazzled by my new image: the costumes, the tur-

quoise and silver jewelry. It seemed to please him. Far from
disappointed in the woman who'd scorched his heart, he seemed
glad to see me.

We spent the days together, sightseeing, Disneyland. Celia
Cruz was in town and when i reached his front steps, having
spent an afternoon on my own, he waited for me at the door with
a gardenia for my hair. We're going dancing tonight, mi linda,
oh yes! We were fast, lively partners, recalling instinctively how
one turned, the other followed.

One night, we faced each other. The only light in the studio
came from the neon sign across the street. It was an odd sensation, becoming at once the "prodigal wife" and the woman he
didn't yet know.

i wanted to respect his bachelor life, didn't answer the phone,
kept away from the windows when a woman incessantly buzzed
the door downstairs.

He'd met a woman, whom he described, as loving him as only
a woman who loves for the first time can. (Ho-Ho!) What was *i*
doing there then? i asked. i was the unattainable, came the answer.

i'd left him because i thought i was fighting a society in which
men and women entangled their relationships with untruths.

He, of course, had a different version of the tale. He had
been loving and i, ungrateful. To add to this, he'd painted a
picture of his estranged wife to his lover of a godless devil. It
explained his inability to make a commitment to her, and most of
all, the reason for his impotency when they met.

Impotency? The word fell into the night air and hung suspended like a black spirit. i hadn't remembered. Had i really left
him because of that?

To go on, *she,* his lover, had managed to cure him of his
affliction with her loyalty, insatiable passion. After this discussion, we slept like two sexless children, locked together to keep
the nightmares at bay.

So now you see why weeks later, after i'd left him, when my
body began to undergo suspicious changes, there was no way i
would get back in touch with him. i'd made a vow once as my
womb was attacked, and i kept it.

i worked until the week Vittorio was born.

When i was pregnant, i went to an exhibition of prints by an
Italian artist. They were sardonic, comical, erotic, melancholy. i

didn't know the artist, didn't meet him or ever see him, but the work touched a certain cord in those months. His name was Vittorio somebody.

Vittorio, my son, is too new to life to know of my isolation. As far as he is concerned, i am the world, there to satisfy every need and whim. There are days when i want to shout for all to see the miracle. i confess, they carry me through those when i want to deny his existence.

Teresa

LETTER FORTY

Mi agridulce Alicia,

i don't know if words will help give promise that at the end of a journey, one comes home for one purpose: to start over.

For days, despite the numbness i've felt by your news, i've tried to determine the precise moment when Abdel gave up. The last time i saw him was only a few months ago when you were both here to christen Vittorio.

It's been said once a Catholic, always a Catholic. Perhaps it was a superstitious idiosyncracy that provoked me to want Vittorio baptized.

A practical sense of reality warned me that my child required spiritual insurance of another's protection if something were to happen to his mamita. Since our views on parenting are similar i was pleased when you consented to be his godmother, particularly because we already know you're not a religious-type person.

i appreciated it all the more knowing your modest lifestyle and that you lived with a man, who for many sad reasons wasn't able to support himself.

Abdel's ex-wife, you said, was dynamic: a dancer, schoolteacher, a political activist. She'd been left with the children, the brownstone, new furniture, and all the payments. On alternate weekends he had the children, brought them to you, aroused maternal instincts you would rather not acknowledge.

i think Abdel would've liked to have been a great artist, or at least, just have done something worth noticing. While he thought of this he drank beer and left his dirty underwear lying around.

He could be gentle, concerned about a woman's frustrations, listened quietly to your complaints. He was without malice. You loved him. But you didn't give him courage, which is what he sought from you from the beginning.

Forgive me for speaking this way when you're most likely castigating yourself in your own reflections. But don't.

Abdel was a weak man, Alicia, and he had already sucked you dry of more than what a child can demand of its mother. Unlike the child, the man never wanted to grow independent. On the contrary, his dependency became greater, the demands, the pathetic sulking when he didn't have his way more frequent.

When you were both here, he was in one of his rare adult moods, good humored, not anything like what you'd written. He poured with affection for Vittorio, cooing and coddling, delighted with every gesture and silly expression. He took care of the baby when we went shopping. It even seemed that he was disappointed when his sitter's services were no longer required and the mother insisted on putting her baby to sleep or, simply, holding him herself.

We were in the kitchen one day. i cooked and Vittorio was in his chair. Abdel picked the baby up and began to play with him, never tired of the child's self-preoccupation. "Look, Alicia! Look how the baby's holding on to my finger!" Abdel pretended to try to break free of the baby's hold.

"Yeah! This boy's gonna grow up to be a wrestling champ!" Abdel smiled in the baby's face. "How'd you like to come to live with us, Vito? Wouldn't you like that? Your ol' mama wouldn't miss you. You come home and be my little boy, huh?"

From the corner of my eye i saw you lean against the wall, arms crossed. Something dark crossed your mind.

"Hey, Alicia, I got an idea. How 'bout if you and me have a

little baby of our own, just like this one here. Look at 'im, babe! Tell me you can resist that face . . . !"

My Vittorio's existence had intrigued you but he opened a Pandora's box of unspoken sentiments.

Abdel didn't know!
He had brought his children
to you
children he had not been responsible for
and expected you to be mother
to them as well as to him. Abdel didn't know
that even if things got better, his head clearer you were never
going to have a baby. Never.

The following day at the airport, i gave you a list of general instructions if Vittorio should ever become yours: he should be taught to look after himself, mend his own clothes, cook, clean up and do his share. He should be allowed to do whatever it was that little boys liked to do but he should also be sensitive . . .

You smiled and gave me a peck on the cheek without looking into my eyes. i watched until you disappeared down the ramp. Next to you went a man you tried to teach all the things i had just told you Vittorio must learn if he was to grow up to be a decent companion to a woman.

When Abdel realized you were aware of his parasitic tendencies, that you wouldn't succumb indefinitely but that the day drew near when he would be thrown out, he resented you. He wouldn't let you rest so easily with pulling him away from your apron strings. You'd remember how you cruelly washed your hands of him. Heartless woman.

First came the slap, so unexpected you were stunned rather than
. hurt.

Then came the day he tried to shove you down the stairs, but you held on firmly and struggled until the super came and broke it up.

Not succeeding in physically intimidating you, he lashed out another way. He destroyed your works, smashed a ceramic sculpture, smeared a watercolor with hot coffee. It was time for him to go, you said, pack his stuff and just leave. You didn't want to fight anymore, there was nothing to discuss.

Once, he threw a fit, lay on the kitchen floor and pounded on it with hands and feet. You stepped right over him and went out for a walk.

There was one thing left to do.

He would get even.

He would make you pay.

You'd be sorry. And how you would cry.

i'm sorry too, Alicia.

i don't know how many layers it takes to strip away a person's dignity before he finds himself in that naked state, ugly and useless. i don't know why he hated you so or loved himself so little that he could have left you with a self-portrait of such macabre perversity. i have heard of those who'd insisted on company.

You came home from class that afternoon. Wednesdays you also had an evening class but you preferred coming home to eat rather than having the cafeteria food. Sometimes, Abdel brought you something to eat, but not lately. You walked home lingeringly. It was a nice day for New York, not muggy, but warm with a cool breeze against your face, hair. Perhaps Abdel might be up for a bike ride.

You'd fix lunch and speak gently to him. It would be a day like the ones you shared before . . . Someday, maybe next Sunday, you'd take the train out to see your parents and introduce them to Abdel. Maybe not, but you'd bring up the idea to him and to your mother. If she could reason with your father, then maybe . . .

to hell with your father. You'd have your mother over Sunday. That would please Abdel. He would be sure then that you weren't going to up and leave him, or throw him out just like that. Yeah, a bike ride would be nice.

From the corner you saw the ambulance, a crowd formed on the stoop. You thought of the old woman on the floor below your apartment, the violent couple across the hall. You quickened your pace and broke through the crowd. You heard the super identify you to the police, she lives there, and wondered for an instant why he bothered. One, two, three, four, five flights of stairs and still you hadn't met up with whatever had happened. The old lady peeked from a crack in the door, the tenants from across the hall had stopped either descending or ascending between the fourth and fifth floors, clinged to each other. One tried to smile as you went past, a thin hand reached out as if to stop you but timidly pulled back.

Just before you climbed the last

flight of stairs, from the landing where the abstract hung, you
saw the door wide open and heard unfamiliar voices.
This is only a dream.

> *Abdel, tell me you didn't do something*
> *to make me feel sorry for you.*

Abdel, you have the prettiest eyes I've ever seen.
Oh yeah, I know I teased you about Rodney and his yellow eyes
but yours, black as the most peaceful sleep, floating, adrift
on the ocean, oh yes, Abdel, you are special.

> *Come to me, come on, baby, oh ·*

just like this . . .

"Do you live here, miss?" Heart pounds. You have reached
the top landing. The man, with a cigarette, moves aside.
Don't move aside, don't let me in.

> *Go away. This is only*

a dream. We don't want you here. Leave us alone now.
We'll be all right.

"Are you all right, ma'am?" There's a tug at your elbow, you
pull away.

> Your eyes are pinned to the rumpled

figure on the kitchen floor. Abdel lies perfectly still. His eyes
haven't been closed and they stare out at you like those glass ones
in stuffed deer heads. Abdel's head is bathed in crimson, rests on
a crimson pillow of his own blood.   *Is Abdel dead?*
He wasn't dead this morning when you left, was he? He sat right there at
the window, looking out at the morning sun. You didn't even know he had
a gun.

"I didn't even know he had a gun," you said to no one in
particular.

"Will you come with us now, ma'am?"

"I didn't even know he had a gun . . ."

> *I DIDN'T KNOW YOU*

HAD A GUN! I DIDN'T . . . KNOW . . . !

> *MOTHER OF GOD, HELP!*

TERESA . . . ? ABDEL, YOU SON OF A BITCH!

Motherfucker, why didn't you just leave?

About the Author

Ana Castillo is a poet, novelist, essayist, editor, and translator. Her work has been widely anthologized in the United States, Mexico, and Europe, and she has received numerous fellowships and awards, including an NEA fellowship in poetry. In addition to *The Mixquiahuala Letters*, her first novel, she is the author of various works, including four volumes of poetry, the novel *Sapogonia*, and a collection of feminist essays entitled *Massacre of the Dreamers: Reflections on Mexican-Indian Women in the U.S.; 500 Years After the Conquest*. She holds a doctorate in American studies.